TED HUGHES

How the Whale

Illustrated by George Adamson

ff

faber and faber

First published in 1963
by Faber and Faber Limited
Bloomsbury House
74–7 Great Russell Street
London WC1B 3DA
This paperback edition first published in 2011

Photoset by Parker Typesetting Service, Leicester
Printed in England by CPI Bookmarque, Croydon, UK

© Ted Hughes, 1963
Illustrations © Faber and Faber Limited, 1963

The right of Ted Hughes to be identified as author of this work
has been asserted in accordance with Section 77 of the Copyright,
Designs and Patents Act 1988

A CIP record for this book
is available from the British Library

ISBN 978–0–571–27420–8

2 4 6 8 10 9 7 5 3 1

For Frieda and Nicholas

Contents

Long ago when the world was brand new, before animals or birds, the sun rose into the sky and brought the first day.

The flowers jumped up and stared round astonished. Then from every side, from under leaves and from behind rocks, creatures began to appear.

In those days the colours were much better than they are now, much brighter. And the air sparkled because it had never been used.

But don't think everything was so easy.

To begin with, all the creatures were pretty much alike – very different from what they are now. They had no idea what they were going to become. Some wanted to become linnets, some wanted to become lions, some wanted to become other things. The ones that wanted to become lions practised at being lions – and by and by, sure enough, they began to turn into lions. So, the ones that wanted to become linnets practised at being linnets, and slowly they turned into linnets. And so on.

But there were other creatures that came about in other ways . . .

Why the Owl Behaves as it does

When Owl became an Owl, the first thing he discovered was that he could see by night. The next thing he discovered was that none of the other birds could.

They could see only by day. They knew it was no use trying to see by dark night, so at every grey dusk they closed their eyes and slept until the grey dawn. They had been doing this for so long, they had forgotten what the dark was.

Owl thought about this. Then he went to the other birds and said: 'I know a country where there are farms, but no farmers. You may eat when and where you please. There are no guns, no bird-scarers, no men. I will take you there if you like.'

Every day, Man killed large numbers of the birds as they were feeding in the fields. They said:

'This sounds like a safe, peaceful country, made for birds. Let us go with Owl.'

Owl smiled to himself.

'Good,' he said. 'Now, as we have no passports, we shall have to cross the frontier by night, when no one can see us. We shall leave at dusk and should be there by dawn.'

When dusk came, Owl led all the birds to a rabbit hole on the hill.

'Hold each other's hands,' he cried. 'I will lead you.'

All the rabbits that lived on the hill ran up to see what new game the birds were playing. Owl led the way down into the dark hole.

'Is this night, then?' whispered the linnets in the pitchy darkness of the hole.

'Hmm,' said the crows. 'So this is night.'

It was so dark down the hole that the birds couldn't even see their own beaks. Each one clung to the wing of the bird in front and followed blindly. Owl led them to and fro in the loops and twists of the hole for about five minutes. By that time, the birds, who were not at all used to walking, felt as if they had been travelling for hours.

'Is it much further?' cried the swallows. 'Oh, our poor little feet!'

At last Owl shouted:

'Halt, while I see if it's all clear up ahead.'

He popped his head out of the rabbit hole and looked around. It was darker than when they had entered the hole a few minutes before, but it was not yet quite night. There was still a pale light in the west.

'Here we are!' he cried then. 'Over the border, just as dawn is breaking.'

And he led the birds out into the open. All the rabbits ran up again and sat, one ear up and one ear down, watching the birds with very puzzled expressions.

'Is this the new country?' asked the birds, and they crept close together, looking round at the almost dark landscape.

'This is it,' said Owl. 'And that is dawn you can see breaking in the east.'

The birds had quite lost their bearings in the dark underground, and the landscape was now too dark to recognize as the one they knew so well by day. They believed everything that Owl said.

Owl led them off the hill and down towards a farm.

'But it seems to be getting darker,' said the doves suddenly.

'Ah, I am glad you noticed that,' said Owl. 'That is something I forgot to tell you. In this country, day is darker than dawn.'

He smiled to himself, but the birds looked at each other in dismay.

'But what about the nights?' they cried. 'If day is darker than dawn, how dark are the nights?'

Owl stopped and looked at them. They couldn't see his face, but they could tell that he was very serious.

'Night here,' he said, 'is so dark, so terribly dark, that it is impossible for a mere bird to survive one glimpse of it. There is only one thing to do if you want to keep alive. You must close your eyes as tight as you can as soon as the dark of the day begins to turn grey. You must keep them closed until I awake you at grey dawn. One peep at the dark, and you are dead birds.'

Then, without another word, he led them into the stackyard of the farm.

The farm lights were out. The farmer was sleeping. The farm was silent.

'Here you are,' said Owl. 'Just as I promised. Now feed.'

The birds scratched and pecked, but by now it was too dark to see a thing. At last they learned to find the grains by feeling with their feet. But it was slow work.

Meanwhile Owl sat on the corner of the barn, overlooking the stackyard. Whenever he felt like it, he dropped down and snatched up a nightingale or a willow-warbler. In the pitch dark, the rest of the birds were no wiser. 'This is better than rats and mice and beetles,' said Owl, as he cleaned the blood from his beak. By the time the first grey light showed in the sky, Owl was fuller than he had ever been in his life.

He gave a shout:

'Here comes the grey of dusk. Hurry, hurry! We must get to our beds and close our eyes before the terrible dark comes.'

Tumbling over each other and bumping into things, the birds ran towards his voice. When they were all gathered, he led them to a nearby copse which was full of brambles.

'Here is good roosting,' said Owl. 'I will awaken you at dawn.'

And so, in the grey of dawn, which Owl had told them was the grey of dusk, the birds closed their eyes. All that bright day they stood in groups under the brambles, their eyes tightly closed. Some of them were too frightened to fall asleep. Not one of them dared to open an eye. One look at that darkness, Owl had said, and you are dead birds.

Owl dozed happily in the dark hollow of a tree. His trick was working perfectly. He was very pleased with himself. No more mice and rats and beetles for him.

At dusk he gave a shout.

'Here is dawn,' he told the birds. 'Back to our feeding.'

And he led them back to the farm where everything happened as the night before.

In this way, Owl grew fat and contented, while the other birds grew wretched.

They grew tired of scraping in the dark stackyard. Sometimes they swallowed a grain, but as often it was a cinder. The farm cocks and hens that picked the stackyard over from end to end all day long had not left much for the birds.

And when they fell asleep, they were terrified lest they have a dream, open their eyes without thinking, and catch a glimpse of the deadly darkness. It was a great strain. Owl was continually warning them of the danger.

'One peep at that darkness,' he kept saying, 'and you are dead birds.'

If only one little bird had peeped, for only one second, with only one eye, he would have seen that there was no such thing as deadly darkness. He would have seen the sun, and the countryside he

7

knew so well. But Owl made sure that none ever did.

The birds grew thin. Their feathers began to fall out. Their feet ached with stumbling about in the darkness, and their wings ached with never being used. They did not like the new country.

They complained among themselves.

At last one dusk, when Owl awoke them with his usual cry: 'Dawn!' they all went up to him and told him they could stand it no longer.

'Please lead us back to our own country,' said the birds.

Owl was worried. He wanted to keep the birds in his power. He didn't want to go back to eating rats, mice and beetles.

Then he had an idea.

'Yes,' he said. 'You are right. This is a fine country, and not dangerous. But, as you say, it is hard to make a living here. Let us find the hole by which we came and return to our own country.'

He led them up to the rabbit warren on the hill. It was almost dark.

'Here are the birds playing that game again,' said the rabbits, and they all ran up to stare.

'Now,' said Owl to the birds. 'It was one of these holes, but just which one I cannot remember. Can any of you remember?'

'I think it might have been this one,' said Cuckoo.

'Or perhaps this one,' said Jenny Wren.

'Let us try them all,' said Owl.

Most of the birds didn't dare to enter the holes lest

they get lost. The ones that did were soon up again saying:

'This one comes out here.'

And:

'This one comes out here.'

Owl pretended to be distressed.

'We have lost our way back, and it is all my fault. Oh dear!' he cried. Then he made his voice sound very brave, as he said:

'As we are here for good, let us make the best of it.'

And he led them down to the stackyard for the night's feeding.

So it went on, for almost a year.

At last the birds decided they had had enough. They were too unhappy to go on living.

'This is no life whatsoever,' they said to each other.

'Let us all die bravely, and at once,' said Robin, 'rather than go on dying slowly in this miserable way.'

'We will do that!' cried the storm-cocks. 'Let us all die bravely together, rather than live like this.'

'But how?' said Little Gold-Crested Wren. 'How can we die?'

'Let us open our eyes,' said Robin, 'to the deadly darkness. Owl said that will kill us all.'

The unhappy birds went out with Owl that night for the last time. He led them to the stackyard as usual, and took up his post. But instead of trying to find food, the birds all sat down together in a big close group in the middle of the yard. They had decided what to do. But Owl knew nothing of it. He stared down. Softly, the birds began to sing their old songs.

'What's the matter with you?' cried Owl. 'You'll starve if you don't eat!'

But the birds took no notice of him. They went on singing, in their thin, hungry voices. It was a long time since they had sung. Now they sang very low, and very sadly.

It was a bright night, with a full moon, but Owl couldn't catch a single one of those birds. They were pressed far too closely one against another. He couldn't even pick one from the edge of the group. And they sang all night long.

By dawn Owl was furious.

'Dusk!' he cried. 'Back to the copse! Here comes the deadly dark.'

He was very hungry. But he knew what he would do. He would sneak down on them by broad day, when they were standing under the brambles with their eyes tight shut. Then he would eat his fill. He would have a song-thrush, a yellow-hammer, a greenfinch, and five bluetits –

'Where are you going?' he cried.

Instead of following him back to the copse, the birds had turned up the hill. Following the rising ground, they came at last to the very top. All around them lay the dark landscape. They gathered under the three elm trees there and faced the first grey line that was showing in the East. Then, once more, they began to sing their old songs.

Soon the deadly darkness would begin to spread through the sky. Or so they thought. They stared into the brightening dawn and sang, holding their eyes as wide as they could to catch the first rays of deadly darkness.

Oh, they were so tired of their lives.

To die like this was better than to live as they had been doing, going nowhere but where Owl led them, always in darkness, scraping their feet raw for a few grains.

They sang, and stared into the dawn. Every moment they expected the first killing ray of black to shoot out of the bright east.

At the edge of the field Owl was beating his head with his wings. He knew what the result would be. In a few minutes the sun would rise, and the birds would recognize the landscape round them.

'Come home!' he cried. 'You sillies! You'll all be killed dead as stones. Come home and close your eyes!'

But the birds had no more interest in anything that Owl said. They only wanted to die.

Slowly the sun put its burning red edge into the sky.

Lark gave a shriek. He sprang up into the air.

'It's the sun!' he cried. 'It's real day!'

Slowly the sun rose.

As it rose, the birds flew up into the branches of the elms, dancing on the twigs, and singing till their heads rang.

'It's the sun!' they sang. 'It's real day!'

From under a blackthorn bush at the field's edge, Owl stared in rage. Then he ducked his head, and flew away down the hedge, low over the ground. Even so, the birds saw him.

'He tricked us!' they cried. 'And there he goes! There goes the trickster!'

In a shouting mob, all the birds flocked after Owl. All the way back to his tree they beat him with their wings, and pulled out his feathers. He buried himself deep in his hollow tree.

The birds flew up into the tree top and sang on.

And so it is still.

Every morning the birds sing, and the Owl flies back to his dark hole. When the birds see him, they mob him, remembering his trick. He dare come out only at night, to scrape a bare living on rats, mice and beetles.

How the Whale Became

Now God had a little back-garden. In this garden he grew carrots, onions, beans and whatever else he needed for his dinner. It was a fine little garden. The plants were in neat rows, and a tidy fence kept out the animals. God was pleased with it.

One day as he was weeding the carrots he saw a strange thing between the rows. It was no more than an inch long, and it was black. It was like a black shiny bean. At one end it had a little root going into the ground.

'That's very odd,' said God. 'I've never seen one of these before. I wonder what it will grow into.'

So he left it growing.

Next day, as he was gardening, he remembered the little shiny black thing. He went to see how it was getting on. He was surprised. During the night it had doubled its length. It was now two inches long, like a shiny black egg.

Every day God went to look at it, and every day it was bigger. Every morning, in fact, it was just twice as long as it had been the morning before.

When it was six feet long, God said:

13

'It's getting too big. I must pull it up and cook it.'
But he left it a day.

Next day it was twelve feet long and far too big to go into any of God's pans.

God stood scratching his head and looking at it. Already it had crushed most of his carrots out of sight. If it went on growing at this rate it would soon be pushing his house over.

Suddenly, as he looked at it, it opened an eye and looked at him.

God was amazed.

The eye was quite small and round. It was near the thickest end, and farthest from the root. He walked round to the other side, and there was another eye, also looking at him.

'Well!' said God. 'And how do you do?'

The round eye blinked, and the smooth glossy skin under it wrinkled slightly, as if the thing were smiling. But there was no mouth, so God wasn't sure.

Next morning God rose early and went out into his garden.

Sure enough, during the night his new black plant with eyes had doubled its length again. It had pushed down part of his fence, so that its head was sticking out into the road, one eye looking up it, and one down. Its side was pressed against the kitchen wall.

God walked round to its front and looked it in the eye.

'You are too big,' he said sternly. 'Please stop growing before you push my house down.'

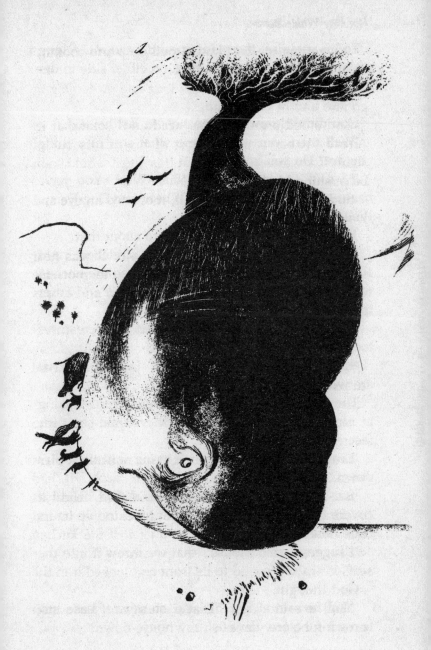

To his surprise, the plant opened a mouth. A long slit of a mouth, which ran back on either side under the eyes.

'I can't,' said the mouth.

God didn't know what to say. At last he said:

'Well then, can you tell me what sort of a thing you are? Do you know?'

'I,' said the thing, 'am Whale-Wort. You have heard of Egg-Plant, and Buck-Wheat, and Dog-Daisy. Well, I am Whale-Wort.'

There was nothing God could do about that.

By next morning, Whale-Wort stretched right across the road, and his side had pushed the kitchen wall into the kitchen. He was now longer and fatter than a bus.

When God saw this, he called the creatures together.

'Here's a strange thing,' he said. 'Look at it. What are we going to do with it?'

The creatures walked round Whale-Wort, looking at him. His skin was so shiny they could see their faces in it.

'Leave it,' suggested Ostrich. 'And wait till it dies down.'

'But it might go on growing,' said God. 'Until it covers the whole earth. We shall have to live on its back. Think of that.'

'I suggest,' said Mouse, 'that we throw it into the sea.'

God thought.

'No,' he said at last. 'That's too severe. Let's just leave it for a few days.'

After three more days, God's house was completely flat, and Whale-Wort was as long as a street.

'Now,' said Mouse, 'it is too late to throw it into the sea. Whale-Wort is too big to move.'

But God fastened long thick ropes round him and called up all the creatures to help haul on the ends.

'Hey!' cried Whale-Wort. 'Leave me alone.'

'You are going into the sea,' cried Mouse. 'And it serves you right. Taking up all this space.'

'But I'm happy!' cried Whale-Wort again. 'I'm happy just lying here. Leave me and let me sleep. I was made just to lie and sleep.'

'Into the sea!' cried Mouse.

'No!' cried Whale-Wort.

'Into the sea!' cried all the creatures. And they hauled on the ropes. With a great groan, Whale-Wort's root came out of the ground. He began to thresh and twist, beating down houses and trees with his long root, as the creatures dragged him willy-nilly through the countryside.

At last they got him to the top of a high cliff. With a great shout they rolled him over the edge and into the sea.

'Help! Help!' cried Whale-Wort. 'I shall drown! Please let me come back on land where I can sleep.'

'Not until you're smaller!' shouted God. 'Then you can come back.'

'But how am I to get smaller?' wept Whale-Wort, as he rolled to and fro in the sea. 'Please show me how to get smaller so that I can live on land.'

God bent down from the high cliff and poked Whale-Wort on the top of his head with his finger.

'Ow!' cried Whale-Wort. 'What was that for? You've made a hole. The water will come in.'

'No it won't,' said God. 'But some of you will come out. Now just you start blowing some of yourself out through that hole.'

Whale-Wort blew, and a a high jet of spray shot up out of the hole that God had made.

'Now go on blowing,' said God.

Whale-Wort blew and blew. Soon he was quite a bit smaller. As he shrunk, his skin, that had been so tight and glossy, became covered with tiny wrinkles. At last God said to him:

'When you're as small as a cucumber, just give a shout. Then you can come back into my garden. But until then, you shall stay in the sea.'

And God walked away with all his creatures, leaving Whale-Wort rolling and blowing in the sea.

Soon Whale-Wort was down to the size of a bus. But blowing was hard work, and by this time he felt like a sleep. He took a deep breath and sank down to the bottom of the sea for a sleep. Above all, he loved to sleep.

When he awoke he gave a roar of dismay. While he was asleep he had grown back to the length of a street and the fatness of a ship with two funnels.

He rose to the surface as fast as he could and began to blow. Soon he was back down to the size of a lorry. But soon, too, he felt like another sleep. He took a deep breath and sank to the bottom.

When he awoke he was back to the length of a street.

This went on for years. It is still going on.

As fast as Whale-Wort shrinks with blowing, he grows with sleeping. Sometimes, when he is feeling very strong, he gets himself down to the size of a motor-car. But always, before he gets himself down to the size of a cucumber, he remembers how nice it is to sleep. When he wakes, he has grown again.

He longs to come back on land and sleep in the sun, with his root in the earth. But instead of that, he must roll and blow, out on the wild sea. And until he is allowed to come back on land, the creatures call him just Whale.

How the Fox Came to be where it is

Now there were two creatures that were very much alike. But one was rusty-red, with a thick tail, neat legs, and black pricking ears, while the other was just plain shaggy black and white. They were both rivals for the job of guarding Man's farm from the other animals.

The shaggy black and white one was called Foursquare, and he wanted the job because he longed to lie beside Man's fire on the cold nights. The rusty-red one was called Slylooking, and he wanted the job for a very different reason. He loved cabbages, and the only way to get near Man's cabbages was by pretending to guard them.

This rivalry went on for a long time, and still neither of them had got the job. At last Man told them to settle the matter between themselves, within a week, or else he would have to employ a bird.

'It is plain,' said Slylooking, 'that we must put our problem before a committee.'

'Very well,' said Foursquare. 'I'm glad to see you so fair-minded. I suggest that we let the cows decide it. They ponder a great deal.'

'But about what?' cried Slylooking, pretending to be alarmed. 'Scenery! That's what they ponder about. They gaze at the scenery and it looks as if they're pondering, and so they get a great name as thinkers. They're no use for important, deep problems such as ours.'

'Then whom do you suggest?'

Now Slylooking had a secret plan. 'I suggest,' he said with a sly look, 'I suggest the hens. They sit on their perches, without a move, and in the dark and all night long – they have nothing else to do but think. They have no scenery to distract them. Besides, they have a fine chairman, the cock, who keeps them in very good order.'

'Then hens it is,' said Foursquare generously.

The hens listened carefully to the problem and promised to give their answer by eleven o'clock next morning.

Foursquare found a soft warm place between hay-ricks and settled down for the night. But Slylooking could not sleep. He had much too much to do.

First of all he went to Rabbit-becomer. He said that he had discovered a whole store of cabbages which, he knew, Rabbit loved as much as he himself did.

'Where? Where?' cried Rabbit, hopping from one leg to the other.

'Well,' said Slylooking with a sly look, 'they're in the garden inside Man's farm. If only I could dig a hole as well as you can, I'd have them in a jiffy. Now if you. . .'

His voice sank to a whisper.

Away went Rabbit with Slylooking to dig the hole.

21

After an hour's hard digging, under Slylooking's directions, Rabbit burst up through the floor of the hen-house. In a flash, Slylooking slipped past him. The hens shouted and flapped in the darkness for a moment – then snickity-snackity! Fox had gobbled the lot.

'These are lively cabbages,' said Rabbit, blinking in the darkness.

'They're the wrong ones!' cried Slylooking, pretending to be very alarmed. 'Run for your life, they don't taste like cabbages at all. I think they're cocks and hens.'

At this, Rabbit ran, and behind him, laughing silently, ran Slylooking, away down the long burrow.

Next morning Slylooking roused Foursquare, and together they went along to the hen-house to hear the decision. Slylooking kept his head turned so that Foursquare should not see his smile. He knocked loudly on the hen-house door. When there was no answer, he pretended to look very surprised.

'They must be still deep in thought,' he said, as he knocked again. Still there was no answer, and with a puzzled frown at Foursquare, he opened the door.

And immediately jumped back.

'Murder! Murder!' he cried. 'Oh, look at the poor hens!'

Foursquare ran in. Nothing was to be seen but piles of feathers and a fresh rabbit hole in the middle of the floor.

'Who's been here?' cried Slylooking, pointing at the burrow.

'Well, that looks like Rabbit's work,' said Foursquare.

'The villain!' cried Slylooking. 'Does he hope to get away with this?'

And away he went down the long burrow, almost choking with laughter.

He found Rabbit crouched in the end of a side-shoot, still trembling, terrified by what Slylooking had persuaded him to do. Without a word, Slylooking bundled him into a sack and carried him back to Man.

'Here's the villain who murdered all your poor chickens,' he said. 'Put him in your pot.'

Man was delighted. He was so pleased, in fact, that he employed Slylooking on the spot to guard his farm, and told him to go and tell Foursquare the decision.

And so Slylooking became the sentry at the farm and was happy among the cabbages. But not for long. He could not get out of his head the way those hens had tasted. One night, as he patrolled the farm, chewing a cabbage leaf, he thought and thought of those hens until he could bear it no longer. There were new hens in the hen-house and Slylooking went straight there.

'Good evening, ladies,' he said as he entered. 'Is everything all right?' Once he had the door closed behind him he chose the fattest hen and snap! she was gone. The others looked at him in alarm.

'What will Man say when we tell him?' they cried.

Slylooking smiled, and snuppity, snippity, snoppity, snap! There was nothing left but a pile of feathers.

Next morning, Man just couldn't understand it. But he put new hens in the hen-house. Slylooking swore he had never heard a thing.

That night he visited the hen-house again.

And so every night for a week. He couldn't resist it. And each time he had to gobble up every single hen lest any be left to tell Man what he had been up to. He quite lost his taste for cabbage leaves.

One evening, as he was going for a stroll in the fields, he met Foursquare.

'What are you doing, still snooping round here? Away with you!' he cried. 'I've to guard the farm against such creatures as you.'

Foursquare looked at him steadily and said, 'You have a hen feather in the corner of your mouth.'

Slylooking was furious, but before he could say anything Foursquare had walked away.

Slylooking didn't like Foursquare's remark at all. It looked as if he suspected the truth. So Slylooking decided to play a trick on Foursquare and get rid of him. He went straight to Man.

'I have an idea,' he said, with a sly look, 'that Foursquare is at the bottom of this hen mystery. He is taking his revenge on you for employing me instead of him.'

'Why,' said Man, 'that seems very likely. Certainly he has very fierce teeth. But how are we to catch him?'

'Leave it to me,' said Slylooking. He had another plan already worked out.

Away he went, and finally he found Foursquare sitting on a green hill watching the river.

'Someone is still eating Man's hens,' said Slylooking. 'Will you help us to catch him?'

Now Foursquare was a very honest creature, and when he heard this he was quite ready to believe that Slylooking was not the culprit as he had suspected.

'How are we to do it?' he asked.

'Well,' said Slylooking, 'it isn't clear whether the murderer comes up through the floor of the hen-house, or whether he comes over the farmyard gate and in at the hen-house door. So tonight, while I watch the farm gate, I want you to hide in the hen-house and keep an eye on the floor.'

'Well, that should catch him, whoever it is,' said Foursquare. 'What time shall I come?'

'Come about midnight. I'll let you in,' said Slylooking with a sly look.

A quarter of an hour before midnight Slylooking slipped into the hen-house and had a banquet of hens. Then he went off to meet Foursquare. Foursquare was waiting under the hedge.

'Quickly, quickly!' said Slylooking. 'The murderer may be here any minute. Hurry. Into the hen-house.'

As soon as Foursquare was in the hen-house with the pile of feathers, Slylooking bolted the door and ran for Man.

'I've trapped the murderer!' he cried. 'I've got him!'

Man came running to see who it was.

'Why it's Foursquare. Just as you said. Well done, Slylooking.' Man dragged Foursquare out of the hen-house, tied him to the fence, and ran to fetch his gun.

Slylooking danced round poor Foursquare, looking at him merrily out of his eye-corner and singing:

> '*This is the end of this stor-ee,*
> *Bullets for you and chickens for me.*'

'Oh, is that so!' roared Man's voice. He had returned more quickly than Slylooking had expected. Bang! went his gun, and Bang! But Slylooking was over the wall and three fields away and still running.

There and then Man untied Foursquare and led him into the farm kitchen. He gave him a great bowlful of food and after that a rug to stretch out on at the fireside.

But that night, and every night after it, Slylooking had to sleep in the wet wood. And whenever he came sneaking back to the farm, sniffing for hens, Foursquare would hear him. He would jump up from his rug, barking at the top of his voice, and Man would be out through the door with his gun.

But Slylooking was too foxy to be caught. In fact, he was so foxy that pretty soon nobody called him Slylooking any more. They called him what we call him – plain Fox.

How the Polar Bear Became

When the animals had been on earth for some time they grew tired of admiring the trees, the flowers and the sun. They began to admire each other. Every animal was eager to be admired, and spent a part of each day making itself look more beautiful.

Soon they began to hold beauty contests.

Sometimes Tiger won the prize, sometimes Eagle, and sometimes Ladybird. Every animal tried hard.

One animal in particular won the prize almost every time. This was Polar Bear.

Polar Bear was white. Not quite snowy white, but much whiter than any of the other creatures. Everyone admired her. In secret, too, everyone was envious of her. But however much they wished that she wasn't quite so beautiful, they couldn't help giving her the prize.

'Polar Bear,' they said, 'with your white fur, you are almost too beautiful.'

All this went to Polar Bear's head. In fact, she became vain. She was always washing and polishing her fur, trying to make it still whiter. After a while she was winning the prize every time. The only times any other creature got a chance to win was when it rained. On those days Polar Bear would say:

'I shall not go out in the wet. The other creatures will be muddy, and my white fur may get splashed.'

Then, perhaps, Frog or Duck would win for a change.

She had a crowd of young admirers who were always hanging around her cave. They were mainly Seals, all very giddy. Whenever she came out they made a loud shrieking roar:

'Ooooooh! How beautiful she is!'

Before long, her white fur was more important to Polar Bear than anything. Whenever a single speck of dust landed on the tip of one hair of it – she was furious.

'How can I be expected to keep beautiful in this country!' she cried then. 'None of you have ever seen me at my best, because of the dirt here. I am really much whiter than any of you have ever seen me. I think I shall have to go into another country. A country where there is none of this dust. Which country would be best?'

She used to talk in this way because then the Seals would cry:

'Oh, please don't leave us. Please don't take your beauty away from us. We will do anything for you.'

And she loved to hear this.

Soon animals were coming from all over the world to look at her. They stared and stared as Polar Bear stretched out on her rock in the sun. Then they went off home and tried to make themselves look like her. But it was no use. They were all the wrong colour.

a

They were black, or brown, or yellow, or ginger, or fawn, or speckled, but not one of them was white. Soon most of them gave up trying to look beautiful. But they still came every day to gaze enviously at Polar Bear. Some brought picnics. They sat in a vast crowd among the trees in front of her cave.

'Just look at her,' said Mother Hippo to her children. 'Now see that you grow up like that.'

But nothing pleased Polar Bear.

'The dust these crowds raise!' she sighed. 'Why can't I ever get away from them? If only there were some spotless, shining country, all for me. . .'

Now pretty well all the creatures were tired of her being so much more admired than they were. But one creature more so than the rest. He was Peregrine Falcon.

He was a beautiful bird, all right. But he was not white. Time and again in the beauty contests he was runner-up to Polar Bear.

'If it were not for her,' he raged to himself, 'I should be first every time.'

He thought and thought for a plan to get rid of her. How? How? How? At last he had it.

One day he went up to Polar Bear.

Now Peregrine Falcon had been to every country in the world. He was a great traveller, as all the creatures well knew.

'I know a country,' he said to Polar Bear, 'which is so clean it is even whiter than you are. Yes, yes, I know, you are beautifully white, but this country is even whiter. The rocks are clear glass and the earth is frozen ice-cream. There is no dirt there, no dust, no mud. You would become whiter than ever in that country. And no one lives there. You could be queen of it.'

Polar Bear tried to hide her excitement.

'I could be queen of it, you say?' she cried. 'This country sounds made for me. No crowds, no dirt? And the rocks, you say, are glass?'

'The rocks,' said Peregrine Falcon, 'are mirrors.'

'Wonderful!' cried Polar Bear.

'And the rain,' he said, 'is white face powder.'

'Better than ever!' she cried. 'How quickly can I be there, away from all these staring crowds and all this dirt?'

'I am going to another country,' she told the other animals. 'It is too dirty here to live.'

Peregrine Falcon hired Whale to carry his passenger. He sat on Whale's forehead, calling out the directions. Polar Bear sat on the shoulder, gazing at the sea. The Seals, who had begged to go with her, sat on the tail.

After some days, they came to the North Pole, where it is all snow and ice.

'Here you are,' cried Peregrine Falcon. 'Everything just as I said. No crowds, no dirt, nothing but beautiful clean whiteness.'

'And the rocks actually are mirrors!' cried Polar Bear, and she ran to the nearest iceberg to repair her beauty after the long trip.

Every day now, she sat on one iceberg or another, making herself beautiful in the mirror of the ice. Always, near her, sat the Seals. Her fur became whiter and whiter in this new clean country. And as it became whiter, the Seals praised her beauty more and more. When she herself saw the improvement in her looks she said:

'I shall never go back to that dirty old country again.'

And there she is still, with all her admirers around her.

Peregrine Falcon flew back to the other creatures and told them that Polar Bear had gone for ever. They were all very glad, and set about making themselves beautiful at once. Every single one was saying to himself:

'Now that Polar Bear is out of the way, perhaps I shall have a chance of the prize at the beauty contest.'

And Peregrine Falcon was saying to himself:

'Surely, now, I am the most beautiful of all creatures.'

But that first contest was won by Little Brown Mouse for her pink feet.

How the Hyena Became

One creature, a Wild-Dog-Becomer called Hyena, copied Leopard-Becomer in everything he did.

Leopard-Becomer was already one of the most respected creatures on the plains. He was strong, swift, fierce, graceful, and had the most beautiful spotted skin.

Hyena longed to be like this. He practised walking like him, crouching like him, pouncing like him. He studied his every move. 'I must get it perfect,' he kept saying to himself.

He followed Leopard-Becomer so closely, in fact, that he never had time to go off and kill his own game. So he had to eat what Leopard left. Leopard didn't take at all kindly to Hyena, and often made him wait a long time for the left-overs. In this way Hyena grew used to eating meat that was none too fresh.

Nevertheless, so long as he could keep near Leopard he was satisfied.

Only one thing could take him from Leopard's track, and that was a chance to boast to the wild-dogs.

'You're nothing but a Wild-Dog yourself,' they said. 'Who do you think you are? Putting on all these Leopard airs?'

'Ha ha,' he replied. 'You wait. Watch me and wait. You're in for a surprise. I'll be a leopard yet.'

One morning he awoke to find his skin covered with big spots, almost like a leopard's.

'Joy! Joy!' he cried, and danced about till he was sodden with dew. He ran off to show himself to the wild-dogs. When they saw his spots they all fled, looking back over their shoulders fearfully.

'Ha ha!' cried Hyena. 'So you thought I was Leopard, did you?'

It was a long time before he could persuade them that he really was Hyena. Even so, they never quite trusted him again.

They began to move away quietly whenever they saw him coming.

As for Hyena, he returned to his Leopard-Becoming with a renewed zest.

This went on for many years.

At last, Hyena began to feel impatient.

'Shall I never be a leopard?' he asked himself. 'I'm still not anywhere near as good as Leopard-Becomer. In fact, he picks up new tricks faster than I learn his old ones.'

He ran to the Wild-Dog-Becomers.

'Am I Leopard yet?' he asked.

They peeped back over the skyline behind which they had run at the first sight of him.

'You are not,' they said. 'But you are not Wild-

Dog either, not any more. The Lord knows what sort of a thing you are now.'

Hyena went back to Leopard. For some years he went about in a very disgruntled condition, but still following Leopard. One day he came as close to Leopard as he dared and said:

'Shall I never become a leopard, Leopard?'

Leopard looked at him in disgust.

'You,' he said, 'have already become what you are going to become.'

'And what is that, please?' asked Hyena politely.

'You have become,' said Leopard, 'a Leopard-Follower.'

Hyena retired to a safe distance and thought about this. He became very embittered.

'Very well,' he said at last. 'If I cannot ever be a leopard, that's finished it. I shall go back to being a wild-dog. Leopard is a stupid creature anyway, calling me a Leopard-Follower.'

And he ran back to the wild-dogs. He knew they would run away when they caught sight of him, so while he was still in the distance he began to shout:

'It's me, Hyena. I'm coming back to be one of you. I've finished with Leopard.'

But it was no use. The wild-dogs ran, and faster than Hyena they ran. He chased them as far as he could move, shouting till his throat ached. At last he stood alone, panting, in the middle of a flat, empty, silent plain.

Sadly, he drooped his tail and turned back. He was feeling hungry. Then he remembered that he didn't know how to kill anything. He walked on and on, getting hungrier and hungrier.

Suddenly he stopped, and sniffed. A leopard had killed a gazelle near there a week ago. He found the bones, cracked them, and sucked them. Then, sniffing, he followed the track of the leopard.

This leopard lived under a rock on top of a hill. Hyena made his bed at the bottom of the hill. Whenever Leopard went out hunting Hyena followed him and ate what he left. In this way he lived.

But he was deeply ashamed. He now saw that he was nothing but a Leopard-Follower after all. He became more bitter than ever. He no longer imitated Leopard. His greatest pleasure now was to sit at a safe distance, when Leopard was eating, and make critical remarks in a loud clear voice:

'What a stupid animal you are! How gluttonously you eat! How boorishly you tear the meat! How disgustingly you growl as you chew!'

And between each comment he gave a laugh, a loud mocking laugh, so that all the other animals within hearing would think he was getting the better of Leopard in some way.

'If I cannot be a leopard,' he said to himself, 'then you shall be ashamed of being a leopard.'

Leopard, of course, was much too fine a beast ever to be ashamed of being what he was.

That was as far as Hyena ever got. He is the same still. He follows Leopard from meal to meal, and laughs and laughs, while Leopard gorges himself on the choicest portions of the meat.

Afterwards, when Leopard has eaten his fill and strolled off to sleep, Hyena stops laughing. Then, at dusk, and on bent legs so as not to be seen, he runs in and tears and gulps all night long at the bones and scraps and rags of meat that are left.

How the Tortoise Became

When God made a creature, he first of all shaped it in clay. Then he baked it in the ovens of the sun until it was hard. Then he took it out of the oven and, when it was cool, breathed life into it. Last of all, he pulled its skin on to it like a tight jersey.

All the animals got different skins. If it was a cold day, God would give to the animals he made on that day a dense, woolly skin. Snow was falling heavily when he made the sheep and the bears.

If it was a hot day, the new animals got a thin skin. On the day he made greyhounds and dachshunds and boys and girls, the weather was so hot God had to wear a sun hat and was calling endlessly for iced drinks.

Now on the day he made Torto, God was so hot the sweat was running down on to the tips of his fingers.

After baking Torto in the oven, God took him out to cool. Then he flopped back in his chair and ordered Elephant to fan him with its ears. He had made Elephant only a few days before and was very

pleased with its big flapping ears. At last he thought that Torto must surely be cool.

'He's had as long as I usually give a little thing like him,' he said, and picking up Torto, he breathed life into him. As he did so, he found out his mistake.

Torto was not cool. Far from it. On that hot day, with no cooling breezes, Torto had remained scorching hot. Just as he was when he came out of the oven.

'Ow!' roared God. He dropped Torto and went hopping away on one leg to the other end of his workshop, shaking his burnt fingers.

'Ow, ow, ow!' he roared again, and plunged his hand into a dish of butter to cure the burns.

Torto meanwhile lay on the floor, just alive, groaning with the heat.

'Oh, I'm so hot!' he moaned. 'So hot! The heat. Oh, the heat!'

God was alarmed that he had given Torto life before he was properly cooled.

'Just a minute, Torto,' he said. 'I'll have a nice, thin, cooling skin on you in a jiffy. Then you'll feel better.'

But Torto wanted no skin. He was too hot as it was.

'No, no!' he cried. 'I shall stifle. Let me go without a skin for a few days. Let me cool off first.'

'That's impossible,' said God. 'All creatures must have skins.'

'No, no!' cried Torto, wiping the sweat from his little brow. 'No skin!'

'Yes!' cried God.

'No!' cried Torto.

'Yes!'

'No!'

God made a grab at Torto, who ducked and ran like lightning under a cupboard. Without any skin to cumber his movements, Torto felt very light and agile.

'Come out!' roared God, and got down on his knees to grope under the cupboard for Torto.

In a flash, Torto was out from under the other end of the cupboard, and while God was still struggling to his feet, he ran out through the door and into the world, without a skin.

The first thing he did was to go to a cool pond and plunge straight into it. There he lay, for several days, just cooling off. Then he came out and began to live among the other creatures. But he was still very hot. Whenever he felt his own heat getting too much for him, he retired to his pond to cool off in the water. In this way, he found life pleasant enough.

Except for one thing. The other creatures didn't approve of Torto.

They all had skins. When they saw Torto without a skin, they were horrified.

'But he has no skin!' cried Porcupine.

'It's disgusting!' cried Yak. 'It's indecent!'

'He's not normal. Leave him to himself,' said Sloth.

So all the animals began to ignore Torto. But they couldn't ignore him completely, because he was a wonderfully swift runner, and whenever they held a race, he won it. He was so nimble without a skin

41

that none of the other creatures could hope to keep up with him.

'I'm a genius-runner,' he said. 'You should respect me. I am faster than the lot of you put together. I was made different.'

But the animals still ignored him. Even when they had to give him the prizes for winning all the races, they still ignored him.

'Torto is a very swift mover,' they said. 'And perhaps swifter than any of us. But what sort of a creature is he? No skin!'

And they all turned up their noses.

At first, Torto didn't care at all. When the animals collected together, with all their fur brushed and combed and set neatly, he strolled among them, smiling happily, naked.

'When will this disgusting creature learn to behave?' cried Turkey, loudly enough for everyone to hear.

'Just take no notice of him,' said Alligator, and lumbered round, in his heavy armour, to face in the opposite direction.

All the animals turned round to face in the opposite direction.

When Torto went up to Grizzly Bear to ask what everyone was looking at, Grizzly Bear pretended to have a fly in his ear. When he went to Armadillo, Armadillo gathered up all his sons and daughters and led them off without a word or a look.

'So that's your game, is it?' said Torto to himself.

Then aloud, he said: 'Never mind. Wait till it comes to the races.'

When the races came, later in the afternoon, Torto won them all. But nobody cheered. He collected the prizes and went off to his pond alone.

'They're jealous of me,' he said. 'That's why they ignore me. But I'll punish them: I'll go on winning all the races.'

That night, God came to Torto and begged him to take a proper skin before it was too late. Torto shook his head:

'The other animals are snobs,' he said. 'Just because they are covered with a skin, they think everyone else should be covered with one too. That's snobbery. But I shall teach them not to be snobs by making them respect me. I shall go on winning all the races.'

And so he did. But still the animals didn't respect him. In fact, they grew to dislike him more and more.

One day there was a very important race-meeting, and all the animals collected at the usual place. But the minute Torto arrived they simply walked away. Simply got up and walked away. Torto sat on the race-track and stared after them. He felt really left out.

'Perhaps,' he thought sadly, 'it would be better if I had a skin. I mightn't be able to run then, but at least I would have friends. I have no friends. Besides, after all this practice, I would still be able to run quite fast.'

But as soon as he said that he felt angry with himself.

'No!' he cried. 'They are snobs. I shall go on winning their races in spite of them. I shall teach them a lesson.'

And he got up from where he was sitting and followed them. He found them all in one place, under a tree. And the races were being run.

'Hey!' he called as he came up to them. 'What about me?'

But at that moment, Tiger held up a sign in front of him. On the sign, Torto read: 'Creatures without skins are not allowed to enter.'

Torto went home and brooded. God came up to him.

'Well, Torto,' said God kindly, 'would you like a skin yet?'

Torto thought deeply.

'Yes,' he said at last, 'I would like a skin. But only a very special sort of skin.'

'And what sort of a skin is that?' asked God.

'I would like,' said Torto, 'a skin that I can put on, or take off, just whenever I please.'

God frowned.

'I'm afraid,' he said, 'I have none like that.'

'Then make one,' replied Torto. 'You're God.'

God went away and came back within an hour.

'Do you want a beautiful skin?' he asked. 'Or do you mind if it's very ugly?'

'I don't care what sort of a skin it is,' said Torto, 'so long as I can take it off and put it back on again just whenever I please.'

God went away again, and again came back within an hour.

'Here it is. That's the best I can do.'

'What's this!' cried Torto. 'But it's horrible!'

'Take it or leave it,' said God, and walked away.

Torto examined the skin. It was tough, rough, and stiff.

'It's like a coconut,' he said. 'With holes in it.'

And so it was. Only it was shiny. When he tried it on, he found it quite snug. It had only one disadvantage. He could move only very slowly in it.

'What's the hurry?' he said to himself then. 'When it comes to moving, who can move faster than me?'

And he laughed. Suddenly he felt delighted. Away he went to where the animals were still running their races.

As he came near to them, he began to think that perhaps his skin was a little rough and ready. But he checked himself:

'Why should I dress up for them?' he said. 'This rough old thing will do. The races are the important thing.'

Tiger lowered his notice and stared in dismay as Torto swaggered past him. All the animals were now turning and staring, nudging each other, and turning and staring.

'That's a change, anyway,' thought Torto.

Then, as usual, he entered for all the races.

The animals began to talk and laugh among themselves as they pictured Torto trying to run in his heavy new clumsy skin.

'He'll look silly, and then how we'll laugh.' And they all laughed.

45

But when he took his skin off at the starting-post, their laughs turned to frowns.

He won all the races, then climbed back into his skin to collect the prizes. He strutted in front of all the animals.

'Now it's my turn to be snobbish,' he said to himself.

Then he went home, took off his skin, and slept sweetly. Life was perfect for him.

This went on for many years. But though the animals would now speak to him, they remembered what he had been. That didn't worry Torto, however. He became very fond of his skin. He began to keep it on at night when he came home after the races. He began to do everything in it, except actually race. He crept around slowly, smiling at the leaves, letting the days pass.

There came a time when there were no races for several weeks. During all this time Torto never took his skin off once. Until, when the first race came round at last, he found he could not take his skin off at all, no matter how he pushed and pulled. He was stuck inside it. He strained and squeezed and gasped, but it was no use. He was stuck.

However, he had already entered for all the races, so he had to run.

He lined up, in his skin, at the start, alongside Hare, Greyhound, Cheetah and Ostrich. They were all great runners, but usually he could beat the lot of them easily. The crowd stood agog.

'Perhaps,' Torto was thinking, 'my skin won't

make much difference. I've never really tried to run my very fastest in it.'

The starter's pistol cracked, and away went Greyhound, Hare, Cheetah and Ostrich, neck and neck. Where was Torto?

The crowd roared with laughter.

Torto had fallen on his face and had not moved an inch. At his first step, cumbered by his stiff, heavy skin, he had fallen on his face. But he tried. He climbed back on to his feet and made one stride, slowly, then a second stride, and was just about to make a third when the race was over and Cheetah had won. Torto had moved not quite three paces. How the crowd laughed!

And so it was with all the races. In not one race did Torto manage to make more than three steps, before it was over.

The crowd was enjoying itself. Torto was weeping with shame.

After the last race, he turned to crawl home. He only wanted to hide. But though the other animals had let him go off alone when he had the prizes, now they came alongside him, in a laughing, mocking crowd.

'Who's the slowest of all the creatures?' they shouted.

'Torto is!'

'Who's the slowest of all the creatures?'

'Torto is!' – all the way home.

After that, Torto tried to keep himself out of sight, but the other animals never let him rest. Whenever any of them chanced to see him, they would shout at the tops of their voices:

'Who's the slowest of all the creatures?'

And all the other creatures within hearing would answer, at the tops of their voices:

'Torto is!'

And that is how Torto came to be known as 'Tortoise'.

How the Bee Became

Now in the middle of the earth lived a demon. This demon spent all his time groping about in the dark tunnels, searching for precious metals and gems.

He was hunch-backed and knobbly-armed. His ears draped over his shoulders like a wrinkly cloak. These kept him safe from the bits of rock that were always falling from the ceilings of his caves. He had only one eye, which was a fire. To keep this fire alive he had to feed it with gold and silver. Over this eye he cooked his supper every night. It is hard to say what he ate. All kinds of fungus that grew in the airless dark on the rocks. His drink was mostly tar and oil, which he loved. There is no end of tar and oil in the middle of the earth.

He rarely came up to the light. Once, when he did, he saw the creatures that God was making.

'What's this?' he cried, when a grasshopper landed on his clawed, horny foot. Then he saw Lion. Then Cobra. Then, far above him, Eagle.

'My word!' he said, and hurried back down into his dark caves to think about what he had seen.

He was jealous of the beautiful things that God was making.

'I will make something,' he said at last, 'which will be far more beautiful than any of God's creatures.'

But he had no idea how to set about it.

So one day he crept up to God's workshop and watched God at work. He peeped from behind the door. He saw him model the clay, bake it in the sun's fire, then breathe life into it. So that was it!

Away he dived, back down into the centre of the earth.

At the centre of the earth it was too hot for clay. Everything was already baked hard. He set about trying to make his own clay.

First, he ground up stones between his palms. That was powder. But how was he to make it into clay? He needed water, and there in the centre of the earth it was too hot for water.

He searched and he searched, but there was none. At last he sat down. He felt so sad he began to cry. Big tears rolled down his nose.

'If only I had water,' he sobbed, 'this clay could become a real living creature. Why do I have to live where there is no water?'

He looked at the powder in his palm, and began to cry afresh. As he looked and wept, and looked and wept, a tear fell off the end of his nose straight into the powder.

But he was too late. A demon's tears are no ordinary tears. There was a red flash, a fizz, a bubbling, and where the powder had been was nothing but a dark stain on his palm.

He felt like weeping again. Now he had water, but no powder.

'So much for stone-powder,' he said. 'I need something stronger.'

Then quickly, before his tears dried, he ground some of the precious metal that he used to feed the fire of his eye. As soon as it was powder he wetted it with a tear off his cheek. But it was no better than the stone-powder had been. There was a flash, a fizz, a bubbling, and nothing.

'Well,' he said. 'What now?'

At last he thought of it – he would make a powder of precious gems. It was hard work grinding these, but at last he had finished. Now for a tear. But he was too excited to cry. He struggled to bring up a single tear. It was no good. His eye was dry as an oven. He struggled and he struggled. Nothing! All at once he sat down and burst into tears.

'It's no good!' he cried. 'I can't cry!' Then he felt his tears wet on his cheeks.

'I'm crying!' he cried joyfully. 'Quick, quick!' And he splashed a tear on to the powder of the precious gems. The result was perfect. He had made a tiny piece of beautiful clay. Only tiny, because his tears had been few. But it was big enough.

'Now,' he said, 'what kind of creature shall I make?'

The jewel-clay was very hard to work into shape. It was tough as red-hot iron.

So he laid the clay on his anvil and began to beat it into shape with his great hammer.

He beat and beat and beat that clay for a thousand years.

And at last it was shaped. Now it needed baking. Very carefully, because the thing he had made was very frail, he put it into the fire of his eye to bake.

Then, beside a great heap of small pieces of gold and silver, for another thousand years he sat, feeding the fire of his eye with the precious metal. All this time, in the depths of his eye glowed his little creature, baking slowly.

At last it was baked.

Now came the real problem. How was he going to breathe life into it?

He puffed and he blew, but it was no good.

'It is so beautiful!' he cried. 'I must give it life!'

It certainly was beautiful. All the precious gems of which it was made mingled their colours. And from the flames in which it had been baked, it had taken a dark fire. It gleamed and flashed: red, blue, orange, green, purple, no bigger than your finger-nail.

But it had no life.

There was only one thing to do. He must go to God and ask him to breathe life into it.

When God saw the demon he was amazed. He had no idea that such a creature existed.

'Who are you?' he asked. 'Where have you come from?'

The demon hung his head. 'Now,' he thought, 'I will use a trick.'

'I'm a jewel-smith,' he said humbly. 'And I live in the centre of the earth. I have brought you a present, to show my respect for you.'

He showed God the little creature that he had made. God was amazed again.

'How beautiful!' he kept saying as he turned it over and over on his hand. 'How beautiful! What a wonderfully clever smith you are.'

'Ah!' said the demon. 'But not so clever as you. I could never breathe life into it. If you had made it, it would be alive. As it is, it is beautiful, but dead.'

God was flattered. 'That's soon altered,' he said. He raised the demon's gift to his lips and breathed life into it.

Then he held it out. It crawled on to the end of his finger.

'Buzz!' it went, and whirred its thin, beautiful wings. Like a flash, the demon snatched it from God's finger-tip and plunged back down into the centre of the earth.

There, for another thousand years, he lay, letting the little creature crawl over his fingers and make short flights from one hand to the other. It glittered all its colours in the light of his eye's fire. The demon was very happy.

'You are more beautiful than any of God's creatures,' he crooned.

But life was hard for the little creature down in the centre of the earth, with no one to play with but the demon. He had God's breath in him, and he longed to be among the other creatures under the sun.

And he was sad for another reason. In his veins ran not blood, but the tears with which the demon had mixed his clay. And what is sadder than a tear?

Feeling the sadness in all his veins, he moved restlessly over the demon's hands.

One day the demon went up to the light to compare his little creature with the ones God had made.

'Buzz!' went his pet, and was away over a mountain.

'Come back!' roared the demon, then quickly covered his mouth with his hands, frightened that God would hear him. He began to search for his creature, but soon, frightened that God would see him, he crept back into the earth.

Still his little creature was not happy.

The sadness of the demon's tears was always in him. It was part of him. It was what flowed in his veins.

'If I gather everything that is sweet and bright and happy,' he said to himself, 'that should make me feel better. Here there are plenty of wonderfully sweet bright happy things.'

And he began to fly from flower to flower, collecting the bright sunny sweetness out of their cups.

'Ah!' he cried. 'Wonderful!'

The sweetness lit up his body. He felt the sun glowing through him from what he drank. For the first time in his life he felt happy.

But the moment he stopped drinking from the flowers, the sadness came creeping back along his veins and the gloom into his thoughts.

'That demon made me of tears,' he said. 'How can I ever hope to get away from the sadness of tears? Unless I never leave these flowers.'

And he hurried from flower to flower.

He could never stop, and it was too good to stop.

Soon, he had drunk so much, the sweetness began to ooze out of his pores. He was so full of it, he was brimming over with it. And every second he drank more.

At last he had to pause.

'I must store all this somewhere,' he said.

So he made a hive, and all the sweetness that oozed from him he stored in that hive. Man found it and called it honey. God saw what the little creature was doing, and blessed him, and called him Bee.

But Bee must still go from flower to flower, seeking sweetness. The tears of the demon are still in his veins ready to make him gloomy the moment he stops drinking from the flowers. When he is angry and stings, the smart of his sting is the tear of the demon. If he has to keep that sweet, it is no wonder that he drinks sweetness until he brims over.

How the Cat Became

Things were running very smoothly and most of the creatures were highly pleased with themselves. Lion was already famous. Even the little shrews and moles and spiders were pretty well known.

But among all these busy creatures there was one who seemed to be getting nowhere. It was Cat.

Cat was a real oddity. The others didn't know what to make of him at all.

He lived in a hollow tree in the wood. Every night, when the rest of the creatures were sound asleep, he retired to the depths of his tree – then such sounds, such screechings, yowlings, wailings! The bats that slept upside-down all day long in the hollows of the tree branches awoke with a start and fled with their wing-tips stuffed into their ears. It seemed to them that Cat was having the worst nightmares ever – ten at a time.

But no. Cat was tuning his violin.

If only you could have seen him! Curled in the warm smooth hollow of his tree, gazing up through the hole at the top of the trunk, smiling at the stars,

winking at the moon – his violin tucked under his chin. Ah, Cat was a happy one.

And all night long he sat there composing his tunes.

Now the creatures didn't like this at all. They saw no use in his music, it made no food, it built no nest, it didn't even keep him warm. And the way Cat lounged around all day, sleeping in the sun, was just more than they could stand.

'He's a bad example,' said Beaver, 'he never does a stroke of work! What if our children think they can live as idly as he does?'

'It's time,' said Weasel, 'that Cat had a job like everybody else in the world.'

So the creatures of the wood formed a Committee to persuade Cat to take a job.

Jay, Magpie, and Parrot went along at dawn and sat in the topmost twigs of Cat's old tree. As soon as Cat poked his head out, they all began together:

'You've to get a job. Get a jōb! Get a job!'

That was only the beginning of it. All day long, everywhere he went, those birds were at him:

'Get a job! Get a job!'

And try as he would, Cat could not get one wink of sleep.

That night he went back to his tree early. He was far too tired to practise on his violin and fell fast asleep in a few minutes. Next morning, when he poked his head out of the tree at first light, the three birds of the Committee were there again, loud as ever:

'Get a job!'

Cat ducked back down into his tree and began to think. He wasn't going to start grubbing around in the wet woods all day, as they wanted him to. Oh no. He wouldn't have any time to play his violin if he did that. There was only one thing to do and he did it.

He tucked his violin under his arm and suddenly jumped out at the top of the tree and set off through the woods at a run. Behind him, shouting and calling, came Jay, Magpie, and Parrot.

Other creatures that were about their daily work in the undergrowth looked up when Cat ran past. No one had ever seen Cat run before.

'Cat's up to something,' they called to each other. 'Maybe he's going to get a job at last.'

Deer, Wild Boar, Bear, Ferret, Mongoose, Porcupine, and a cloud of birds set off after Cat to see where he was going.

After a great deal of running they came to the edge of the forest. There they stopped. As they peered through the leaves they looked sideways at each other and trembled. Ahead of them, across an open field covered with haycocks, was Man's farm.

But Cat wasn't afraid. He went straight on, over the field, and up to Man's door. He raised his paw and banged as hard as he could in the middle of the door.

Man was so surprised to see Cat that at first he just stood, eyes wide, mouth open. No creature ever dared to come on to his fields, let alone knock at his door. Cat spoke first.

'I've come for a job,' he said.

'A job?' asked Man, hardly able to believe his ears.

'Work,' said Cat. 'I want to earn my living.'

Man looked him up and down, then saw his long claws.

'You look as if you'd make a fine rat-catcher,' said Man.

Cat was surprised to hear that. He wondered what it was about him that made him look like a rat catcher. Still, he wasn't going to miss the chance of a job. So he stuck out his chest and said: 'Been doing it for years.'

'Well then, I've a job for you,' said Man. 'My farm's swarming with rats and mice. They're in my haystacks, they're in my corn sacks, and they're all over the pantry.'

So before Cat knew where he was, he had been signed on as a Rat-and-Mouse-Catcher. His pay was milk, and meat, and a place at the fireside. He slept all day and worked all night.

At first he had a terrible time. The rats pulled his tail, the mice nipped his ears. They climbed on to rafters above him and dropped down – thump! on to him in the dark. They teased the life out of him.

But Cat was a quick learner. At the end of the week he could lay out a dozen rats and twice as many mice within half an hour. If he'd gone on laying them out all night there would pretty soon have been none left, and Cat would have been out of a job. So he just caught a few each night – in the first ten minutes or so. Then he retired into the barn and played his violin till morning. This was just the job he had been looking for.

Man was delighted with him. And Mrs Man thought he was beautiful. She took him on to her lap and stroked him for hours on end. What a life! thought Cat. If only those silly creatures in the dripping wet woods could see him now!

Well, when the other farmers saw what a fine rat-and-mouse-catcher Cat was, they all wanted cats too. Soon there were so many cats that our Cat decided to form a string band. Oh yes, they were all great violinists. Every night, after making one pile of rats and another of mice, each cat left his farm and was away over the fields to a little dark spinney.

Then what tunes! All night long. . .

Pretty soon lady cats began to arrive. Now, every night, instead of just music, there was dancing too. And what dances! If only you could have crept up there and peeped into the glade from behind a tree and seen the cats dancing – the glossy furred ladies and the tomcats, some pearly grey, some ginger red, and all with wonderful green flashing eyes. Up and down the glade, with the music flying out all over the night.

At dawn they hung their violins in the larch trees, dashed back to the farms, and pretended they had been working all night among the rats and mice. They lapped their milk hungrily, stretched out at the fireside, and fell asleep with smiles on their faces.

How the Donkey Became

There was one creature that never seemed to change at all. This didn't worry him, though. He hated the thought of becoming any single creature. Oh no, he wanted to become all creatures together, all at once. He used to practise them all in turn – first a lion, then an eagle, then a bull, then a cockatoo, and so on – five minutes each.

He was a strange-looking beast in those days. A kind of no-shape-in-particular. He had legs, sure enough, and eyes and ears and all the rest. But there was something vague about him. He really did look as if he might suddenly turn into anything.

He was called Donkey, which in the language of that time meant 'unable to stick to one thing'.

'You'll never become anything,' the other creatures said, 'until you stick to one thing and that thing alone.'

'Become a lion with us,' the Lion-Becomers said. 'You're so good at lioning it's a pity to waste your time eagling.'

And the eagles said: 'Never mind lioning. You

should concentrate on becoming an eagle. You have a gift for it.'

All the different creatures spoke to him in this way, which made him very proud. So proud, in fact, that he became boastful.

'I'm going to be an Everykind,' Donkey cried, kicking up his heels. 'I'm going to be a Lionocerangoutangadinf.'

Half the day he spent on a high exposed part of the plain practising at his creatures where everyone could see him. The other half he spent sleeping in the long grass. 'I'm growing so fast,' he used to say, 'I need all the sleep I can get.'

But Donkey had a secret worry. He had no means of earning his living. He couldn't earn his living as a lion – not when he only practised at lion five minutes a day. He couldn't earn his living as any other creature either – for the same reason.

So he had to beg.

'When you see me grow up into a Lionocerangoutangadinf,' he said, as he begged a mouthful of fish from Otter, 'you'll be glad you helped me when I was only learning.'

And he went off kicking up his heels.

Before long the animals grew tired of his begging. It took them all day to find food enough for themselves. So whenever Donkey came up to them to beg they began to tease him:

'What?' they cried. 'Aren't you the finest, greatest creature in the world yet? What have you been doing with your time?'

This made Donkey furious. He galloped off to a high hill, and there he sat, brooding.

'The trouble is,' he said, 'there's no place among these creatures for somebody with real ambition. But one day – I'll make them stare! I'll be a better lion than lion, a better eagle than eagle, and a better kangaroo than kangaroo – and all at the same time. Then they'll be sorry.'

All the same, he wished he could earn his living without having to beg.

As he sat, he heard a long sigh. He looked around. He hadn't noticed that he was so near Man's farm. He looked over the fence and saw Man sitting beside a well, with his head resting in his hands. As he looked, Man gave another sigh.

'What's the matter?' asked Donkey.

Man looked up.

'I'm weary,' he said. 'Drawing water from this well is hard work.'

'Hard?' Donkey cried. 'If it's strength you're wanting, here I am. I'm the strongest creature on these plains.'

'But still not strong enough to draw water,' sighed Man.

'Just watch this.' Donkey marched across, took hold of the long pole that stuck out over the well, and began to drag it round. He had often seen Man doing this, so he knew how. Water gushed out of a pipe on to Man's field of corn.

'Wonderful!' cried Man. 'Wonderful!'

Donkey flattened back his ears and pulled all the harder. Man danced around him, crying:

'You're a marvel. Oh, what I wouldn't give to have you working for me.'

As he said that, Donkey got an idea. He stopped.

'If you'll give me food,' he said, 'I'll do this every day for you.'

'It's a bargain!' said Man.

So Donkey started to work for Man.

Only a little bit each morning, mind you. He still spent most of the day out on the plains practising at all his creatures. Then he retired early to sleep in the little shed that Man had made for him – it was dark, out of the wind, and the floor was covered with deep straw. Lovely! There he would lie till it was time for work next morning.

One day Man said to him:

'If you'll work twice as long for me, I'll give you twice as much food.'

Donkey thought:

'Twice as much food means twice as much strength. And if I'm going to be a Lionocerangoutan-gadinf – well – I shall need all the strength that's going.'

So he agreed to work twice as long.

Next day, Man asked him the same again. Donkey agreed. And the next day, and again Donkey agreed. He was now working from dawn to dusk. But the pile of food that Man gave him at the day's end! Well, after eating it, Donkey could do nothing but lie down on his straw and snore.

After about a week of this he suddenly thought:

'Here I am, being gloriously fed. Getting stronger and stronger. But I never have time to practise at my creatures. How can I hope to become a Lionoceran-goutangadinf if I never practise my creatures?'

So what did he do? He couldn't very well practise while he was working. The sight and sound of it would have terrified Man, and Donkey didn't want to lose his job. So he did the only thing he could. He began to practise in his head.

Soon he got to be wonderfully good at this. He could fancy himself any creature he wished – a mountain goat, for instance, leaping among the clouds from crag to crag, or a salmon, climbing a swift fierce torrent – for hours at a time, all in his head. He would quite forget that he was only walking round a well.

Once or twice Man removed him from the well and set him to draw a plough. But donkey was so absorbed in practising at his creatures inside his head that he forgot to turn at the end of the furrow. He went ploughing straight on, through the hedge and into the next field. After this, Man never asked him to do anything but walk around the well, and Donkey was quite contented.

So it went on for several years, and Donkey fancied that he was becoming more and more skilful at his creatures. 'I mustn't be in too great a hurry,' he said to himself. 'I want to be better at everything than every other creature – so a little bit more practice won't hurt.

So he went on. Always staying on with Man for just a little bit more practice inside his head.

'Soon,' he kept saying, 'soon I shall be perfect.'

At last it seemed to Donkey he was nearly perfect.

'A few more days, just a few more days!' Then he would burst out on to the plains, the first Lionoceran-goutangadinf. Within three days, perhaps even within two, the animals would crown him their king – he was sure of that. Just as he was thinking these lovely thoughts he heard a sudden cry. He looked up and saw Man running towards his house, his arms in the air.

At the same moment, over the high fence, came Lion.

Donkey stood, and watched Lion out of the corner of his eye. He tilted one fore-foot carelessly.

Lion stared at him.

At last, making his voice sound as friendly as he could, Donkey said: 'My word, Lion-Becomer, you've changed. Are you Lion yet?'

Lion turned away from him without a word and walked up the path. When he reached Man's house, he stood up on his hind legs and, lifting one paw, like a lion in a coat of arms, began to beat upon the door.

'Throw out your wife and children, Man!' he roared.

Man was crouching under the table inside the house, trembling all over, not daring to breathe.

Finally Lion got tired of beating the door, which was of thick wood and studded with big bolts. He turned round and began to sniff among the out-houses and gardens. He came to Donkey again, who was still propped idly on one foreleg beside the well.

'Hello again, Lion,' said Donkey, and he let his voice be ever such a little bit scornful. 'Your hunting isn't so good, is it? I think I could give you a lesson or two in lioning.'

Lion stared, amazed.

'Now,' thought Donkey, 'now to reveal my true self. Now to reveal what I have made myself after all these years of hard practice.'

And he gave a great leap and roared.

'See!' he cried. 'This is the way!'

And again he leapt and roared, leapt and roared. He became so taken up with his lioning that he completely forgot about Lion.

Now it was years since Donkey had actually tried to leap or roar. He was far too stiff with his years of hard work to leap, and his voice had become stiff as his muscles.

So, though it seemed to him he was doing a wonderful lion, he was really only kicking out his heels stiffly, and sending up a harsh bray.

But he was delighted with himself. He went on, leaping and roaring, as he thought, leaping and roaring, so that his harness clattered, the long pole bounced and banged, and Lion screwed up his eyes in the dust from the kicking-out feet.

At last Lion could stand it no longer. He raised his paw, and with one blow knocked donkey clean into the well. He then jumped back over the fence and returned to his wife, who was waiting on the skyline.

Poor Donkey! When Man hauled him out of the well he was in a sorry state. But he was a wiser Donkey. That night he ate his oats and lay down with a new feeling. No more Lionocerangoutangadinf for him. No more pretending to be every creature.

'It's best to face the truth,' he said to himself, 'and the truth is I'm neither a lion nor an eagle. I am a well-fed, comfortable, hard-working Donkey.'

He could hear the lions roaring hungrily out on the plains, and he thought of the antelopes running hither and thither looking for a safe corner and a place out of the wind. He pushed his head under the warm straw, and smiled into the darkness, and fell into a deep sleep.

How the Hare Became

Now Hare was a real dandy. He was about the vainest creature on the whole earth.

Every morning he spent one hour smartening his fur, another hour smoothing his whiskers, and another cleaning his paws. Then the rest of the day he strutted up and down, admiring his shadow, and saying:

'How handsome I am! How amazingly handsome! Surely some great princess will want to marry me soon.'

The other creatures grew so tired of his vain ways that they decided to teach him a lesson. Now they knew that he would believe any story so long as it made him think he was handsome. So this is what they did:

One morning Gazelle went up to Hare and said:

'Good morning, Hare. How handsome you look. No wonder we've been hearing such stories about you.'

'Stories?' asked Hare. 'What stories?'

'Haven't you heard the news?' cried Gazelle. 'It's about you.'

'News? News? What news?' cried Hare, jumping up and down in excitement.

'Why, the moon wants to marry you,' said Gazelle. 'The beautiful moon, the queen of the night sky. She wants to marry you because she says you're the handsomest creature in the whole world. Oh yes. You should just have heard a few of the things she was saying about you last night.'

'Such as?' cried Hare. 'Such as?' He could hardly wait to hear what fine things moon had said about him.

'Never mind now,' said Gazelle. 'But she'll be walking up that hill tonight, and if you want to marry her you're to be there to meet her. Lucky man!'

Gazelle pointed to a hill on the Eastern skyline. It was not yet midday, but Hare was up on top of that hill in one flash, looking down eagerly on the other side. There was no sign of a palace anywhere where the moon might live. He could see nothing but plains rolling up to the farther skyline. He sat down to wait, getting up every few minutes to take another look round. He certainly was excited.

At last the sky grew dark and a few stars lit up. Hare began to strut about so that the moon should see what a fine figure of a creature was waiting for her. He looked first down one side of the hill, then down the other. But she was still nowhere in sight.

Suddenly he saw her – but not coming up his hill. No. There was a black hill on the skyline, much farther to the East, and she was just peeping silver over the top of that.

'Ah!' cried Hare. 'I've been waiting on the wrong hill. I'll miss her if I don't hurry.'

He set off towards her at a run. How he ran. Down into the dark valley, and up the hill to the top. But what a surprise he got there! The moon had gone. Ahead of him, across another valley, was another skyline, another black hill – and that was the hill the moon was climbing.

'Wait for me! Wait!' Hare cried, and set off again down into the valley.

When he got to the top of that hill he groaned. And no wonder. Far ahead of him was another dark skyline, and another hill – and on top of that hill was the moon standing tiptoe, ready to fly off up the sky.

Without a pause he set off again. His paws were like wings. He ran on the tops of the grass, he ran so fast.

By the time he got to the top of this hill, he saw he was too late. The moon was well up into the sky above him.

'I've missed her!' he cried. 'I'm too late! Oh, what will she think of me!'

And he began leaping up towards her, calling:

'Moon! Moon! I'm here! I've come to marry you.'

But she sailed on up the black sky, round and bright, much too far away to hear. Hare jumped a somersault in pure vexation. Then he began to listen – he stretched up his ears. Perhaps she was saying terrible things about him – or perhaps, yes, perhaps flattering things. Perhaps she wanted to marry him much too much ever to think badly of him. After all, he was so handsome.

All that night he gazed up at the moon and listened. Every minute she seemed more and more beautiful. He dreamed how it would be, living in her palace. He would become a king, of course, if she were a queen.

All at once he noticed that she was beginning to come down the other side of the sky, towards a black hill in the West.

'This time I'll be waiting for her,' he cried, and set off.

But it was just the same. When he got to the top of the hill she was no longer there, but on the farther hill. And when he got to the top of that, she was on the next. And when he got to that, she had gone down behind the farthest hills.

Hare was furious with himself.

'It's my own fault,' he cried. 'It's because I'm so slow. I must be there on time, then I shan't have to run after her. To miss the chance of marrying the moon, and becoming a king, all out of pure slowness!'

That day he told the animals that he was courting the moon, but that the marriage day was not fixed yet. He strutted in front of them, and stroked his fur – after all, he was the creature who was going to marry the moon.

He was so busy being vain, he never noticed how the other creatures smiled as they turned away. Hare had fallen for their trick completely.

That night Hare was out early, but it was just the

same. Again he found himself waiting on the wrong hill. The moon came over the black crest of a hill on the skyline far to the East of him. Hill by hill, he chased her into the East over four hills, but at last she was alone in the sky above him. Then, no matter how he leapt and called after her, she went sailing on up the sky. So he sat and listened and listened to hear what she was saying about him. He could hear nothing.

'Her voice is so soft,' Hare told himself.

He set off in good time for the hill in the West where she had gone down the night before, but again he seemed to have misjudged it. She came down on the hilly skyline that was further again to the West of him, and again he was too late.

Oh, how he longed to marry the moon. Night after night he waited for her, but never once could he hit on the right hill.

Poor Hare! He didn't know that when the moon seemed to be rising from the nearest hill in the East or falling on to the nearest hill in the West, she was really rising and falling over the far, far edge of the world, beyond all hills. Such a trick the creatures had played on him, saying the moon wanted to marry him.

But he didn't give up.

Soon he began to change. With endlessly gazing at the moon he began to get the moonlight in his eyes, giving him a wild, startled look. And with racing from hill to hill he grew to be a wonderful runner. Especially up the hills – he just shot up them. And from leaping to reach her when he was too late, he came to be a great leaper. And from listening and listening, all through the night, for what the moon was saying high in the sky, he got his long, long ears.

How the Elephant Became

The unhappiest of all the creatures was Bombo. Bombo didn't know what to become. At one time he thought he might make a fairly good horse. At another time he thought that perhaps he was meant to be a kind of bull. But it was no good. Not only the horses, but all the other creatures too, gathered to laugh at him when he tried to be a horse. And when he tried to be a bull, the bulls just walked away shaking their heads.

'Be yourself,' they all said.

Bombo sighed. That's all he ever heard: 'Be yourself. Be yourself.' What was himself? That's what he wanted to know.

So most of the time he just stood, with sad eyes, letting the wind blow his ears this way and that, while the other creatures raced around him and above him, perfecting themselves.

'I'm just stupid,' he said to himself. 'Just stupid and slow and I shall never become anything.'

That was his main trouble, he felt sure. He was much too slow and clumsy – and so big! None of the other creatures were anywhere near so big. He searched hard to find another creature as big as he was, but there was not one. This made him feel all the more silly and in the way.

But this was not all. He had great ears that flapped and hung, and a long, long nose. His nose was useful. He could pick things up with it. But none of the other creatures had a nose anything like it. They all had small neat noses, and they laughed at his. In fact, with that, and his ears, and his long white sticking-out tusks, he was a sight.

As he stood, there was a sudden thunder of hooves. Bombo looked up in alarm.

'Aside, aside, aside!' roared a huge voice. 'We're going down to drink.'

Bombo managed to force his way backwards into a painful clump of thorn-bushes, just in time to let Buffalo charge past with all his family. Their long black bodies shone, their curved horns tossed, their tails screwed and curled, as they pounded down towards the water in a cloud of dust. The earth shook under them.

'There's no doubt,' said Bombo, 'who they are. If only I could be as sure of what I am as Buffalo is of what he is.'

Then he pulled himself together.

'To be myself,' he said aloud, 'I shall have to do something that no other creature does. Lion roars and pounces, and Buffalo charges up and down bellowing. Each of these creatures does something that no other creature does. So. What shall I do?'

He thought hard for a minute.

Then he lay down, rolled over on to his back, and

waved his four great legs in the air. After that he stood on his head and lifted his hind legs straight up as if he were going to sunburn the soles of his feet. From this position, he lowered himself back on to his four feet, stood up and looked round. The others should soon get to know me by that, he thought.

Nobody was in sight, so he waited until a pack of wolves appeared on the horizon. Then he began again. On to his back, his legs in the air, then on to his head, and his hind legs straight up.

'Phew!' he grunted, as he lowered himself. 'I shall need some practice before I can keep this up for long.'

When he stood up and looked round him this second time, he got a shock. All the animals were round him in a ring, rolling on their sides with laughter.

'Do it again! Oh, do it again!' they were crying, as they rolled and laughed. 'Do it again. Oh, I shall die with laughter. Oh, my sides, my sides!'

Bombo stared at them in horror.

After a few minutes the laughter died down.

'Come on!' roared Lion. 'Do it again and make us laugh. You look so silly when you do it.'

But Bombo just stood. This was much worse than imitating some other animal. He had never made them laugh so much before.

He sat down and pretended to be inspecting one of his feet, as if he were alone. And, one by one, now that there was nothing to laugh at, the other animals walked away, still chuckling over what they had seen.

'Next show same time tomorrow!' shouted Fox, and they all burst out laughing again.

Bombo sat, playing with his foot, letting the tears trickle down his long nose.

Well, he'd had enough. He'd tried to be himself, and all the animals had laughed at him.

That night he waded out to a small island in the middle of the great river that ran through the forest. And there, from then on, Bombo lived alone, seen by nobody but the little birds and a few beetles.

One night, many years later, Parrot suddenly screamed and flew up into the air above the trees. All his feathers were singed. The forest was on fire.

Within a few minutes, the animals were running for their lives. Jaguar, Wolf, Stag, Cow, Bear, Sheep, Cockerel, Mouse, Giraffe – all were running side by side and jumping over each other to get away from the flames. Behind them, the fire came through the tree-tops like a terrific red wind.

'Oh dear! Oh dear! Our houses, our children!' cried the animals.

Lion and Buffalo were running along with the rest.

'The fire will go as far as the forest goes, and the forest goes on for ever,' they cried, and ran with sparks falling into their hair. On and on they ran, hour after hour, and all they could hear was the thunder of the fire at their tails.

On into the middle of the next day, and still they were running.

At last they came to the wide, deep, swift river.

They could go no further. Behind them the fire boomed as it leapt from tree to tree. Smoke lay so thickly over the forest and the river that the sun could not be seen. The animals floundered in the shallows at the river's edge, trampling the banks to mud, treading on each other, coughing and sneezing in the white ashes that were falling thicker than thick snow out of the cloud of smoke. Fox sat on Sheep and Sheep sat on Rhinoceros.

They all set up a terrible roaring, wailing, crying, howling, moaning sound. It seemed like the end of the animals. The fire came nearer, bending over them like a thundering roof, while the black river swirled and rumbled beside them.

Out on his island stood Bombo, admiring the fire which made a fine sight through the smoke with its high spikes of red flame. He knew he was quite safe on his island. The fire couldn't cross that great stretch of water very easily.

At first he didn't see the animals crowding low by the edge of the water. The smoke and ash were too thick in the air. But soon he heard them. He recognized Lion's voice shouting:

'Keep ducking yourselves in the water. Keep your fur wet and the sparks will not burn you.'

And the voice of Sheep crying:

'If we duck ourselves we're swept away by the river.'

And the other creatures – Gnu, Ferret, Cobra, Partridge, crying:

'We must drown or burn. Goodbye, brothers and sisters!'

It certainly did seem like the end of the animals.

Without a pause, Bombo pushed his way into the water. The river was deep, the current heavy and fierce, but Bombo's legs were both long and strong. Burnt trees, that had fallen into the river higher up and were drifting down, banged against him, but he hardly felt them.

In a few minutes he was coming up into shallow water towards the animals. He was almost too late. the flames were forcing them, step by step, into the river, where the current was snatching them away.

Lion was sitting on Buffalo, Wolf was sitting on Lion, Wildcat on Wolf, Badger on Wildcat, Cockerel on Badger, Rat on Cockerel, Weasel on Rat, Lizard on Weasel, Tree-Creeper on Lizard, Harvest Mouse on Tree-Creeper, Beetle on Harvest Mouse, Wasp on Beetle, and on top of Wasp, Ant, gazing at the raging flames through his spectacles and covering his ears from their roar.

When the animals saw Bombo looming through the smoke, a great shout went up:

'It's Bombo! It's Bombo!'

All the animals took up the cry:

'Bombo! Bombo!'

Bombo kept coming closer. As he came, he sucked up water in his long silly nose and squirted it over his back, to protect himself from the heat and the sparks. Then, with the same long, silly nose he reached out and began to pick up the animals, one by one, and seat them on his back.

'Take us!' cried Mole.

'Take us!' cried Monkey.

He loaded his back with the creatures that had hooves and big feet; then he told the little clinging things to cling on to the great folds of his ears. Soon he had every single creature aboard. Then he turned and began to wade back across the river, carrying all the animals of the forest towards safety.

Once they were safe on the island they danced for joy. Then they sat down to watch the fire. Suddenly Mouse gave a shout:

'Look! The wind is bringing sparks across the river. The sparks are blowing into the island trees. We shall burn here too.'

As he spoke, one of the trees on the edge of the island crackled into flame. The animals set up a great cry and began to run in all directions.

'Help! Help! Help! We shall burn here too!'

But Bombo was ready. He put those long silly tusks of his, that he had once been so ashamed of, under the roots of the burning tree and heaved it into the river. He threw every tree into the river till the island was bare. The sparks now fell on to the bare torn ground, where the animals trod them out easily. Bombo had saved them again.

Next morning the fire had died out at the river's edge. The animals on the island looked across at the smoking, blackened plain where the forest had been. Then they looked round for Bombo.

He was nowhere to be seen.

'Bombo!' they shouted. 'Bombo!' And listened to the echo.

But he had gone.

He is still very hard to find. Though he is huge and strong, he is very quiet.

But what did become of him in the end? Where is he now?

Ask any of the animals, and they will tell you:

'Though he is shy, he is the strongest, the cleverest, and the kindest of all the animals. He can carry anything and he can push anything down. He can pick you up in his nose and wave you in the air. We would make him our king if we could get him to wear a crown.'

Holding Mister Nibbles close to his chest, he made his way inside the house, picked up the phone and tapped out Bright's number.

After a couple of rings, Bright answered. 'I don't want any double glazing,' he said tetchily, 'and I've already got a fitted kitchen, thanks, and I don't care that I've won a fabulous prize ...'

'Bright!' John yelled into the phone, 'It's me! Shut up and listen!'

He blurted out his story. This took quite a long time as he kept leaving bits out and having to go back to explain. Eventually, he finished. 'What can I do?' he moaned.

'How long has it been in the snow?'

'Don't say *it*!' John shouted into the receiver. 'It isn't an *it*, it's a *he*. It's Mister Nibbles!'

'I think you're bringing emotions into this situation,' answered Bright in a very flat voice.

'Of course I am! That's because I *am* emotional. I've killed Mister Nibbles!'

'You're not being very positive about this.'

'I can't see anything to be positive about!' John pointed out.

'Did you know that in China, the word for "crisis" is the same as the word for "opportunity"?'

John held the receiver at arm's length and stared at it. He put it back to his ear.

'Thank you for sharing that information with me at this time,' he said bitterly, 'but you're not being much help!'

'All right. Listen to me very carefully. Everything depends on you following my instructions to the letter. Put it, I mean him, in a box, pack snow around him and put the box into your freezer.'

'What for?' asked John. 'Are you trying to make Mister Nibbles into hamster-flavour ice cream?'

'Sarcasm isn't going to help,' said Bright in a hurt voice.

John made an effort to pull himself together. 'Sorry, I'm feeling upset,' he said more calmly. 'Why do I have to put him in the freezer?'

'No time to explain,' Bright snapped. 'Trust me. I'll be round as quickly as I can.'

The line went dead.

John put the receiver down and sighed. Then he began to do exactly what Bright had told him. He placed the lifeless Mister Nibbles into a plastic ice-cream tub, went outside and gathered up some snow. He placed the snow around Mister Nibbles and put him in the freezer. Then he sat down and sobbed.

Fifteen minutes later, Bright arrived carrying an insulated container full of ice packs.

Wordlessly, John took the ice-cream tub with the lifeless body of Mister Nibbles from the freezer and handed it to Bright. He grimaced as Bright transferred Mister Nibbles into the container and shut the lid.

'Don't worry, leave this to me,' Bright said. 'I need to work quickly.'

'But what are you going to …?'

'Later!' Bright opened the door and stepped into the snow-swirling night.

Back in the kitchen, John shut Mister Nibbles' cage door and ran his fingers along the metal bars. Zzzringgggggg!

He reached into his pocket and brought out Ms Session's list of instructions. Her blood-red warning stood out.

> '<u>DO NOT</u> LET VERNON BRIGHT
> NEAR MISTER NIBBLES!
> OR ELSE …!'

A terrible thought struck John. Until now, he'd been acting on instinct; he had no idea why he'd phoned Bright, except that these days he always turned to Bright in a crisis. But he couldn't have said what he thought Bright might be able to do.

Now he started to think. What *could* Bright do? Why did he want Mister Nibbles? Why had he told John to keep the body cold?

'Cold stops tissue from decomposing quickly,' Bright had said.

John felt himself go as cold as Mister Nibbles in the freezer. Horrible images flashed across his mind.

'What did you do to the tortoise? Put wheels on it?'

'No experiments on living things, I promise. Quite the reverse.'

'The secret of life itself ...'

'Oh no,' groaned John.

What had he done?! He had to get Mister Nibbles back from Bright!

CHAPTER FIVE

Missing: Retrieved Dead

Prrrp – prrrp … prrrp – prrrp … prrrp – prrrp …

'Come on, come on, come on!'

John bit his lip as he listened to Bright's phone ringing. His stomach churned with a nameless dread. Surely Bright wouldn't try to …? John shook his head. He knew Bright would try almost anything. He hardly ever thought about the consequences of the experiments he did.

Bright's phone suddenly clicked into life.

'Bright? Listen, don't do anything to Mister Nibb …' John tailed off as he realized he was listening to an answerphone message.

'You have reached the telephone of Vernon Bright – and his family, but nobody ever calls *them*.

I'm very busy. If you want to sell me something, go away. You can leave a message after the tone if you like, but it had better be something important and I probably shan't bother to pick it up anyway.'

'Bip … bip … bip … bip … bip … bip … bip … beeeeeeeep!'

Furiously, John slammed the phone down, grabbed his jacket and raced off into the night.

Half an hour later, John skidded to a stop in the doorway to Dodgy Dave's warehouse, just as Dave was locking up for the night.

'Vernie?' drawled Dave in reply to John's frantic enquiries. 'Sure I seen him. Quite a while back. I reckon he should be home by now.'

'He isn't.' John was gasping for breath. 'I've been there … I rang the bell for … at least ten … minutes …'

'Waaaal, I couldn't rightly say where he'd be then. He never said where he was goin'. Just came in here and took away all kindsa crazy stuff.'

John gave a squeak of dismay. 'What sort of crazy stuff?'

Dave looked put out. 'Waaal, lemme see now – auto spares, and some old open-contact switches;

you know, the kind you see in the mad scientist's lab in horror films.'

John felt his knees go weak. 'Horror films?'

'Sure, you know.' Dave pointed dramatically and roared, 'Throw the switch, Igor!' He then twisted his body grotesquely, and lisped, 'Yeth, marthter.' He straightened up. 'Did I ever tell you about the time I met Boris Karloff?'

John sat down suddenly. His legs didn't seem to want to hold him up any more.

'Oh, yeah, and a defibrillator.'

John stared at him. 'What's a defribillator?'

'De – fib – rill – a – tor,' said Dave, very clearly. 'You musta seen them on hospital shows.' He pantomimed a medic about to resuscitate a patient whose heart had stopped. He rubbed two imaginary pads together and ordered, *'Clear!'* Then he placed the pads on an unseen chest and his hands jerked as the electric current sent the non-existent patient into a violent spasm. 'Kapow!'

'Oh dear,' said John faintly.

Snow was still falling as John trudged disconsolately homewards. He'd thought of camping on Bright's doorstep until he returned, but the idea held little appeal. For one thing, Bright might already be inside, and John had known him to stay in the lab for days on end when he was really interested in something.

On his way home, he passed a pet shop. It was one of the bigger sort. The original shop, 'Pets' Paradise', had expanded and taken over the shops on either side. The three shop fronts now had signs reading 'Furry Friends', 'Feathered Friends' and

'Fishy Friends,' according to their contents, though 'Fishy Friends' now had a sign in the window reading '... AND SNAKES TOO!' John guessed that the snakes weren't particularly friendly.

He suddenly had a brainwave. Maybe he could buy a hamster that looked just like Mister Nibbles! The shop was still open. He hurried inside and headed for the 'small animals' section. Hope faded as John realized that none of the hamsters for sale looked anything like Mister Nibbles. Not one of them would fool Ms Session for a moment.

The shop bell tinkled, and a policeman walked in. The shop owner who came forward to meet him was a fussy little man with glasses, a bow tie and a hairpiece that wasn't fooling anybody. He seemed ill at ease.

'Mr Veasey?' said the policeman. 'I had a call – about some missing animals?'

John gasped in horror. Was he talking about Mister Nibbles? Surely Ms Session couldn't have found out and reported him to the police already? He ducked down behind the hamster cages and listened.

'Well, yes,' said the shop owner. 'One doesn't like to bother ... I mean, I know how busy you ...

it's hardly the crime of the century, I know, but ...'

The policeman gave a barely audible sigh and flipped open his notebook. 'I'll just take a few details, shall I? What's missing then?'

The pet-shop owner peered at him with watery eyes and said, 'Rats!'

The policeman looked scandalized. 'I beg your pardon, sir?'

'And mice. Two of each.'

'Oh, I see.' The policeman's brow cleared. He wrote in his notebook, speaking the words as he scribbled. 'Two ... rats ... two ... mice ...' He stopped writing and gave a chuckle. 'Pity they weren't three blind mice, eh, sir? Then we'd know who we were looking for, wouldn't we?'

Mr Veasey blinked at him. 'Would we?'

'Well, it'd be the Farmer's Wife, wouldn't it? Open-and-shut case. We'd only have to find the carving knife and we'd have her bang to rights.' The policeman laughed uproariously. Mr Veasey stared at him in bewildered silence.

The policeman coughed. 'Yes, well ... I suppose there wasn't a lock on the cage?'

Mr Veasey looked blank. 'What cage?'

'The one with the rats and mice in.'

'Oh, they weren't in a cage. There wouldn't have been any point, you see. They were dead.'

It was the policeman's turn to look blank. 'Dead?'

'Oh yes, quite dead. We'd just got them from the breeding centre. We were going to feed them to the snakes.'

The policeman looked pained. Some kid, desperate for a pet, nicking a few furry creatures, fair enough – but some ghoul snatching dead animals? That was getting into territory that the policeman absolutely did not want to know about.

'Have you noticed anybody coming into the shop acting suspiciously?' he asked.

Mr Veasey's brow furrowed with concentration. 'Well, no, I …' Suddenly he snapped his fingers. 'Yes, now I come to think of it. Some boy with dreadfully untidy hair' (here, Mr Veasey patted his own toupee with ill-judged pride) 'came in and asked me if I had any dead animals for sale. I said I had some, but they weren't for sale, and …' Mr Veasey's watery eyes widened as the penny dropped. 'You don't suppose he might have …?'

John didn't wait to hear what the policeman

supposed. It couldn't be worse than what John himself supposed. Bright had collected equipment from Dodgy Dave's. Now, evidently, he was prowling round the local pet shops collecting spare parts ...

'We're losing him! We're losing him! Five ccs of streptocortoviacene!'

The nurse hurriedly thrust a needle through the cork top of a small medicine bottle, and drew a syringeful of colourless liquid. She passed this to the white-coated figure, who was desperately applying artificial respiration to the inert body on the operating table.

The injection seemed to have no effect. The man in the white coat whipped out a stethoscope and listened to the patient's chest. Throwing the instrument aside, he bent down and applied an ear to the same spot. With a cry of dismay, he began furiously to massage the unmoving chest.

'Breathe! Breathe, blast you!'

The nurse shook her head and slowly removed her surgical mask. 'He's gone.'

Choking back a sob, the man tore off his surgical coat and ran a distraught hand through his hair.

'Why? Dear Lord in heaven, why?'

The nurse gave a sigh. 'Don't blame yourself. There was nothing more you could have done.'

'I know – it's just that I hate losing a patient ...'

The nurse patted his arm. 'Don't be too hard on yourself. After all, he must have been six if he was a day.'

'Six!' The man shook his head in despair.

'Well, that's pretty old for a guinea pig.'

As the vet and the nurse left the operating theatre, they didn't notice a shadowy figure slip in through the door, and reach out towards the unmoving bundle of fur on the table ...

Outside, the shadowy figure with spiky hair slipped through the snow-filled streets. Its coat pockets bulged with insulated containers.

It stepped into an alley and disappeared from view.

CHAPTER SIX

The Secret of Life

The next day, John was determined to go round to Bright's house and find out what he was up to, no matter what. However, his mother had other ideas. It was the last Saturday before Christmas, and John was dragged off on a shop-till-you-drop search for presents. So it was not until late afternoon that he hammered on Bright's door.

'I know you're in there!' he shouted. 'Let me in!' He rang the bell again. And again. He kept on ringing it for over twenty minutes. He was freezing cold, but that didn't matter. He had to see Bright and find out what exactly was going on.

'I'm not going away!' he yelled and jabbed at the

doorbell once again. This time he kept his finger pressed firmly on the button.

Eventually, the door opened.

John pointed an accusing finger at Bright. 'What're you ... uh?'

Bright was dressed in a green surgical gown and hat. A mask hung round his neck. John gulped. There were small reddish-brown stains on the gown. John hoped they weren't what he thought they were.

Bright's hair was even more of a mess than usual. His face was lined. He had dark blotches round his eyes. He looked like a panda after a really bad night out.

'Steady on!' he said. 'You'll do yourself a mischief.'

'The only person here doing mischief is you,' snapped John. 'What have you done with Mister Nibbles?'

Bright's mouth creased into a tired smile. 'I think you'd better come in out of the snow.' He closed the door behind John. 'Now, whatever is the matter?'

John took a deep breath. 'Someone stole some dead rats from "Pets' Paradise" yesterday.

Someone who just happened to fit your description.' John looked Bright in the eye. 'Was it you?'

Bright looked indignant. 'I offered to pay for them.'

'It's still stealing! Anyway, why do you need dead rats?' John eyed Bright's green surgical gown with deep distrust. 'And why are you dressed like that?'

'I can explain everything,' Bright said. 'Come down to the lab ...'

Bright's lab looked even more chaotic than normal. The computer printer was almost buried under what looked like printouts from the Internet. On a bench top there were several books. John could make out their titles: *Microbiology*, *Advanced Organ Systems*, *A-Z of Veterinary Medicine* and *Needlework for Beginners*.

Also lying on the bench was Frankenstein's notebook. It was open.

As he looked around the room, it dawned on John that Bright had rearranged the lab. Standing in the middle of the room was a table. It was surrounded by the sort of complicated equipment

John had seen on TV hospital-dramas, and covered with a white tablecloth, which had a horribly suggestive hump in the middle. Waves of foreboding began to wash around John's body.

Bright closed the lab door and rubbed his hands together. 'I've solved the problem,' he announced.

'Which problem?' said John icily. 'The problem that you've gone crackers or the problem that Ms Session is going to kill me once she finds out that I've let you near Mister Nibbles?'

'I shall ignore your caustic comments,' said

Bright. 'I have solved the problem of Mister Nibbles.' He moved to the middle of the lab and took hold of a corner of the tablecloth. Like a magician, Bright whisked off the cloth. 'Da daaa!'

John stared at the sight that confronted him. It was appalling, but he was too horrified to be ill.

The body of a hamster lay lifeless on the table. But it wasn't the Mister Nibbles that John recognized. This hamster was covered in stitches, which joined together odd bits of fur. What lay on the table looked as if a furry patchwork quilt had been stretched over a plasticine model of a hamster made by a particularly ham-fisted child. It looked lopsided, and deformed and … wrong. Bits stuck out of it. It bulged in strange places.

'Is that Mister Nibbles?' quavered John.

'Mostly,' replied Bright. 'It's about ninety per cent Mister Nibbles. Of course, some of his organs and other tissues were damaged beyond repair, so I had to replace those with bits of rat, mouse and guinea pig. What do you think?' Bright asked, admiring his handiwork.

John shook his head. The feeling of nausea was threatening to overwhelm him. He looked at Bright in disgust. 'I think you're sick. You're sicker than a big bowl full of sick with sick topping. You are a sick, sick, sick, sick, sick person, do you know that?'

Bright frowned. 'Am I missing something? Is there a problem?'

John slumped across a bench, held his head in his hands and moaned. 'I'm dead, Session will kill me.' He looked up mournfully. 'What have you done to Mister Nibbles?'

'I've rebuilt him!' exclaimed Bright. 'You wouldn't believe the work I've had to do. Some of it is quite revolutionary! I've had to research all kinds of things such as ...'

John shook his head and switched off. Bright had stolen dead animals and used them to make some sort of monstrous animal jigsaw puzzle. And here he was talking and boasting about it as though it was a perfectly normal way to behave. Was he even on the same planet?

'... and that was when I realized I could actually do it!'

'Oh, really? That's good,' replied John, wondering whether he had enough money saved up to emigrate.

'Of course, Frankenstein's notes are all about the

70

human body, but a hamster's body is very similar.'

John stared at him. 'Oh, come on! Even I know that a human being is THIS BIG ...' John stood on tiptoe and spread his arms wide, '... and a hamster is THIS BIG.' He held his thumb and forefinger very close together.

Bright gave an exasperated sigh. 'I mean their bodies work the same way. I had to think about every system and the job each one does to make sure that Mister Nibbles could be put back together in one piece.'

'More like lots of pieces stuck together,' John pointed out acidly.

Bright wasn't listening. 'It was stitching mostly.' He indicated the complicated mass of apparatus standing around the table. 'Of course, I had to use a microscope and microsurgical techniques.'

'Of course,' John agreed weakly.

'The digestive system was straightforward enough – just a matter of sewing a lot of guts up.'

'Oh, please!' protested John.

'Then there was the respiratory system. Remember, that's what Ms Session was going on about when she showed us the lungs and you ...'

'Yes, I know I fainted!' snapped John. 'It really

71

gets on my nerves the way everyone reminds me about it!'

Bright grimaced. 'The nervous system – I had real difficulties with that, I can tell you. That and the endocrine system. That's all to do with hormones and chemicals.' He held up Frankenstein's notebook. 'That's where good old Frankenstein came in very handy!'

Warning bells began to ring in John's mind.

'The skeletal system was simplicity itself,' Bright continued. 'Though by the time your cat had finished with Mister Nibbles, there were a few bones that were beyond repair! I had to be a bit creative there.'

John looked at the misshapen thing on the table and shuddered.

'Then it was a simple task of sorting out the muscular system and the circulatory system. The heart and blood were easy, thanks to good old Frankenstein!' Bright suddenly looked cagey. 'I didn't bother with the ninth system.'

'Why not?' asked John.

'Er that's the … erm, the …' Bright's voice became noticeably quieter, 'the reproductive system. Babies and that sort of thing.'

'Well, I can see that that's something you'd want to steer clear of. You wouldn't want a whole family of Mister Nibbleses.'

There was a mad glint in Bright's eyes. He threw his head back and stretched his arms out wide. 'And now,' he announced in ringing tones, 'I am ready to bring Mister Nibbles back to life!'

There was a short pause.

Followed by a longer one.

Eventually, John slowly stood up, keeping Bright at arm's length. 'You *have* gone completely mad!' he declared. 'You've lost your marbles! You're off your trolley! You're three stitches short of an operation, completely gaga, out to lunch, dippy, daffy, potty, barmy and cracked! You're a stark-raving, one hundred per cent, certifiable NUTCASE!'

'You don't believe I can do it, do you?'

'Brilliantly spotted!' cried John.

Bright stroked Frankenstein's notebook lovingly. 'I can. It's all in here. The secret of life.'

John snatched the book from his hands. 'That's great. The secret of life!' He grabbed Bright by the front of his green coat. 'You've made things a hundred times worse. I could have kept Mister

Nibbles in the freezer, and taken him back to school and said, "Sorry, Ms Session, the cat got him," and shown her, and maybe she'd only have killed me a little bit.' He waved a frantic hand at the monstrosity on the table. 'But how can I show her *that*? She'll know I let you get at him!'

'What you will show her,' said Bright very slowly and seriously, 'is a living, breathing creature, which I shall have returned to life.'

'Get real! You'll never do it.'

'I can do it. Why shouldn't I?'

For a moment, John was nonplussed. Then he remembered a bit from one of their biology lessons. 'Well, for one thing, didn't Session tell us that you can't mix up bits of different animals in one body?'

'Aha,' said Bright. 'You're talking about rejection.'

'Am I?'

'Yes. For instance, if you put the wrong type of blood into your body, your body will reject it and that means big trouble.'

'I'm sure it does,' said John, struggling to keep up with Bright.

'It's pretty much the same with tissue as well.'

John looked puzzled. 'For blowing your nose?'

Bright rolled his eyes. 'No! Tissue, as in body tissue. Cells, muscles, skin.' He glanced at Mister Nibbles' patchwork coat. 'Or fur. The body recognizes that the tissue is different and rejects it, just as it rejects the wrong type of blood.'

'So, what you're saying is, you can't actually bring Mister Nibbles back to life because his body will reject all the other bits you've used to rebuild him!'

A wide grin spread across Bright's face. 'Aha! That's where Frankenstein comes in. He discovered a way to make sure that the body doesn't reject anything that is different. He invented a serum. A sort of magic liquid. But it's not magic, it's science.'

Bright gazed lovingly at the horrible thing on the operating table. 'This liquid is made up of several ingredients that stimulate dormant cells and stop the rejection process.' He reached across to the bench top and picked up a glass bottle, half-filled with a thick amber liquid. He held it up and gently shook it.

'The secret of life,' he whispered. 'This fluid will

persuade Mister Nibbles' body that the new bits I've put in him and on him are really his, so they won't be rejected! What's more, after a transplant, it would take months and months for cells and nerves to grow back, but Frankenstein thought of everything. The serum contains an agent that makes everything grow much more quickly. He was obviously a genius and now I'm going to follow in his footsteps.' Bright paused for a second. 'Its time to bring Mister Nibbles back ...'

Bright wheeled a strange-looking machine over to the table. It seemed to be built around an old fridge and had wires, dials, lights and various switches. It was attached to a car battery. Two coils of electric wire came out of the box. They were connected to two metal teaspoons.

'Good, isn't it?' smirked Bright. 'I made it.'

John stared at the machine. 'I'd never have guessed.'

'I'm glad you're here,' Bright went on. 'I need your help with this bit.'

'I suppose you want me to screw up my face, walk with a limp, talk with a lithp and call myself Igor,' said John sarcastically.

'Why would you want to do that?' asked Bright

in all seriousness. He connected various wires and tubes from the machine to the hamster. 'If it makes you feel better, fine, do it.'

'What do you want me to do?'

'We have to restart Mister Nibbles' body. And the key to that is the heart. We need to get that going by pumping the blood and my ... that is, Frankenstein's ... serum around Mister Nibbles' body.'

Bright plugged the fridge into a bench-socket and switched it on. The motor rattled into life. Bright took the top off his bottle of serum and connected it to tubes coming from the fridge. The fluid passed down a tube into the hamster's body. After a short delay, it began to come out again, into another tube leading back to the bottle.

'Round and round the serum goes,' muttered Bright dreamily, 'and where it stops, no one knows.'

John began to feel very ill.

Bright started up another motor. A tiny bellows on top of the fridge began to pump. Moments later, to John's fascination and horror, the hamster's chest began to move up and down.

Bright began quietly to sing,

'The toe bone connected to the foot bone,
The foot bone connected to the ankle bone,
The ankle bone connected to the leg bone,
The leg bone connected to the knee bone,
Now hear the word of the Lord ...'

Bright turned to John. His eyes were feverish. There was sweat on his forehead. 'Now he's on a life-support machine,' he said. 'All we need is an electric shock to get his heart beating a steady rhythm.'

'You mean you're going to jump start it?' said John weakly. 'Like a car?'

'Sort of. I've put this machine together with a few bits. I did get hold of a proper medical defibrillator, but then I realized it would be too powerful to use on a hamster. It might explode.'

John stared at him. 'The machine?'

'No, the hamster.' Bright connected two crocodile clips from his contraption to a car battery. Bits began to glow and hum.

'Are you sure this is going to be all right?' asked John fearfully.

'Trust me …'

John hated it when Bright said that.

Bright put on a pair of rubber kitchen gloves

and picked up the two spoons. He placed them on Mister Nibbles' body. He nodded towards a switch. 'I need you to flick this power switch when I say so.'

John's finger closed over the switch. He said nervously, 'Mister Nibbles isn't going to explode, is he?'

'Oh no.'

'Good.'

'I'm almost sure.'

'*Almost* sure?!'

'Throw the switch!'

John flicked the switch and instinctively ducked.

The machine began to rock violently from side to side. John watched open-mouthed as it shot out a storm of yellow, red and orange sparks. Blue bolts of electricity crackled through the air. John could see Bright lit up like a photo negative as he held the teaspoons to the hamster's chest. And in the middle of all the hurly burly, Mister Nibbles twitched madly against the straps holding him to the table.

Then the machine exploded.

There was no movement in the lab for quite a long time.

John groaned. He was lying on the lab floor. His hair was standing on end and his face was blackened.

'Bright! Bright!' he called out. 'Are you OK?'

'No problems.' Bright's face was black, too. He was twitching. John crawled over to him and prised the spoons from his hands.

'Ah well, never mind,' said John sadly. 'You did your best. I'll just have to tell Session that ...'

'Eek, eek!'

Bright and John looked at each other, mouths open. They slowly rose and peered over the edge of the table.

Mister Nibbles was struggling against the tiny bonds that held him strapped to the table. The hamster turned and stared at Bright with two beady, baleful black eyes.

'Eek! Eek!'

Bright leapt up and threw his arms in the air.

'It lives! It lives! My creature is alive!'

CHAPTER SEVEN

Follow-That Hamster!

Bright's Creature (the hamster formerly known as Mister Nibbles), stared accusingly into John's eyes, wringing its paws in misery.

'Look at me!' it squeaked wretchedly. 'I'm so ugly.' As it began to weave back and forth, John realized that one of its shoulders was higher than the other. 'Why am I so ugly?' it moaned. 'Oh, Esmerelda! The bells! The bells!'

John made a grab for it, but it skipped out of his reach and away at an astonishing speed. John raced after it, up a series of twisting stairs that seemed never-ending, before emerging at last into a vast belfry. Overhead, bells clanged and roared as the crazed hamster flung itself at the bell ropes, swinging from one to the other like a rodent Tarzan.

'The bells!' it squeaked. 'The bells!'

The bells rang and rang in John's ears …

He woke up in a cold sweat. The telephone was shrilling urgently. John stared round at the sitting room. He must have fallen asleep in front of the TV. No wonder! He'd hardly slept a wink last night after his session with Bright and that horror on the operating table …

Rubbing his eyes, John reached for the phone. 'Hello?' he grunted.

Bright's voice, sounding urgent and strained, crackled tinnily in his ear. 'You'd better get over here right away. I think we have a problem.'

Suddenly wide awake, John slammed the receiver down and left the room at a dead run.

Although it was still early, the last remains of daylight were fading from the sky. The hard frost of the previous night had given the packed snow an icy gloss. As John ran, and slipped and slithered through the darkening streets, the first flakes of fresh snow began to fall.

John found Bright pacing up and down the kitchen.

'What's happened?' he gasped.

Bright stopped pacing. He glanced nervously at the steel door, which led to the cellar and to his laboratory.

'I'm not sure,' he said. 'I was tired to death last night and I slept in today. I only got up a couple of hours ago. Then I didn't go down to the lab for a bit. I was ...'

'Scared?' suggested John.

'Thinking!' snapped Bright. He crossed his hands over his chest and rubbed his arms, as if he was cold. 'Anyway, after a bit, I went down to the lab, and that's when I found it.'

John stared at him. 'Found what?'

Bright looked at the floor. 'The cage. The one I put Mister Nibbles in.' His voice became unsteady. 'It was broken. Empty.'

'Empty?'

'You heard me. What are you, a parrot?' Anxiety made Bright snappish.

'You mean, somebody broke in and took Mister Nibbles?'

Bright gave John a scornful look. 'Nobody knows

about Mister Nibbles except you and me. Anyway, you know how tight my security system is.'

John gulped. 'Then you're saying ... it's escaped?'

Bright nodded.

John stared around in panic. 'Then where is it now?'

Bright pointed a not-quite-steady finger at the lab door. 'Down there.'

Bright crept down the concrete steps into the lab. Suddenly, with a spine-melting shock, he felt something furry tickle the back of his neck. He spun round with a scream – and saw that John had crept up behind him, carrying a feather duster.

Bright almost choked with anger. He glared at the duster. 'What are you doing with that?' he hissed.

'You said we had to be careful, so I grabbed this to defend myself.'

'What are you going to do? Tickle it to death?'

John looked sheepish. 'It was all I could find.'

Seething with a mixture of fear and exasperation, Bright turned and continued down the steps.

The lab was full of equipment, stacked all over the place. John was uncomfortably aware of how many dark corners this made. Mister Nibbles' cage was lying on its side. As Bright peered nervously into the shadows, John turned the cage over. He was shocked to see that several of the bars had been bent back. It looked as if something had pushed very hard – from the inside.

'Bright,' he croaked, 'come and look at …'

'I know,' snapped Bright. 'I've seen it.'

'But a hamster isn't strong enough to do this kind of damage, is it?'

Bright cautiously peered round the side of a machine. 'A normal hamster isn't, no.'

'Then how …?'

'I don't know yet! Stop jabbering for a minute and let me think!' Bright suddenly gave an exclamation and reached down to the floor. John held his breath. Had Bright found Mister Nibbles?

But when Bright straightened up, he was holding only an empty sack.

'This is weird,' he said to himself.

John felt as if his brain was about to snap. 'You've just made a creature out of a hamster and some other bits, and brought it back to life. *That*'s weird. *This*,' he grabbed the limp object from Bright and shook it, 'is a sack!'

Bright turned a haunted face to John. 'What's weird is, it was full last night.'

John suddenly felt shivery. 'Full? Of what?'

'Hamster food. I bought loads.'

'But a hamster couldn't eat …'

'… that much food in a few hours,' Bright finished. 'I know.'

John looked around the lab again. As his gaze swept over Horace's cage, he drew his breath in sharply. 'What have you done to Horace?' he demanded.

Horace was hanging from the roof of the cage, clenching the bars with all four paws in a death grip. The guinea pig's eyes were wide. His teeth were chattering. He was gibbering with fright.

'I haven't done anything to him! Something else has!' Bright's voice was hoarse. 'All the evidence points to one conclusion.'

'And that is …?'

Bright began to back away towards the cellar steps. 'What we're dealing with isn't exactly a hamster any more. It's strong. It's hungry. And it's big.'

John's throat had gone very dry. 'How big?'

There was a scrabbling sound from a dark corner. Bright signalled John to be quiet, and picked up a metre rule from his workbench. Creeping forward, he poked it cautiously into the shadows.

There was a loud crunching sound. Bright jerked his hand back. He and John stared in horror at what was left of the metre rule. It was very badly gnawed and only about thirty centimetres long.

Without warning, a dark figure leapt from the shadows. An enraged squeaking filled the lab.

John caught a brief glimpse of bristling whiskers and one enraged black eye as something heavy and covered in fur barrelled into him. He crashed into Bright. As they both lay sprawled, face down on the floor, there was a brief thunder of pounding footsteps as something went past them like a runaway train. Then there was a crash as the cellar door was slammed back into the wall.

John lifted his head. The cellar door was swinging brokenly from one hinge. Of the creature that had attacked them, there was no sign.

Gorgeous was prowling the back alleys near Bright's house. He had chased a rival tomcat over there, earlier in the evening, and stayed to see what else was going down in the neighbourhood.

He sniffed the air. The snow made scenting things difficult, but there was a very strong smell coming from around the next corner. It smelt like … Gorgeous licked his chops … it smelt like the mouse-thing he'd caught a couple of days ago. He'd played with it for a while, until it lay still and wouldn't play any more.

The sound of footsteps came to the cat's sensitive ears. They sounded strange – laboured, and irregular, but heavy. Gorgeous sniffed again. He was puzzled. There were lots of mouse-thing smells, all slightly different. What was more, the smells were very strong, as if whatever was making them was big – *very* big …

Well, whatever it is, Gorgeous thought, I'll sort it out. He pinned his ears back flat to his head, bared his fangs, and hissed.

The bins at the end of the alley were suddenly hurled to either side, as if by an explosion. Something stepped into the light.

Gorgeous blinked. His fur stood on end, from his snarling muzzle to the tip of his bottlebrush tail. He made a sound he intended to be a growl, but which came out more like, 'Uh – oh!'

The creature that had been Mister Nibbles reared up on its back legs and loomed over the terrified cat. Its forearms were curved menacingly. Its black eyes, as big as breakfast bowls, glittered with unutterable fury. It took two lurching steps towards the quivering cat, and roared its defiance.

SQUEEEEEEEEEEEEEEEAAAAAAAAAAAAAA AAAAKKKKKKKKKK!!!

Gorgeous was a tomcat, but he very nearly had kittens.

Yowling with panic, he turned tail on the horribly huge and ferocious mouse-thing, and ran for his life.

Back at the lab, John picked himself up off the floor.

'What …?' His voice came out as a high-pitched squeak. He cleared his throat and started again. 'What was that? It looked like a bear!'

Bright staggered to his feet. 'That was no bear. That was a hamster. Mostly.'

John's eyes widened. 'That size? It couldn't be!'

'Well, it couldn't be anything else.' Bright's voice was sarcastic. 'I don't keep bears down here. I'm sure I would have remembered.'

'But, how …?'

Bright shook his head. 'It must have been my formula.' John looked blank. 'You know, the serum I made to promote cell regeneration and to stop the hamster's body rejecting its new parts?' John nodded. 'Well, it must have a side effect.'

John stared at the wrecked lab. 'You call this a side effect?'

Bright wasn't listening. 'Somehow, my formula isn't just causing the cells to regenerate – it's causing tissue growth in every part of the body. That's why the food bag was empty – nothing can grow without food. And by the look of the thing that just attacked us, that growth is rapid and uncontrollable.'

'Uncontrollable?' John grabbed Bright's arm. 'You mean, it's going to get bigger?'

Bright nodded dumbly.

'How much bigger?'

'I don't know. But I do know this. It's growing all the time, so it's going to be very hungry.'

They panted up the steps and into the kitchen. The back door was hanging off its hinges.

John stared out into the night. 'How are we going to find it?'

'Wait here.' Bright plunged back into the house and emerged a few moments later carrying a powerful electric torch. 'We'll follow its spoor.'

John raised his eyebrows. 'Its what?'

'Its trail, you idiot. It should be easy enough to pick up.'

John followed the shadowy figure of Bright, wavering along behind the torch beam as it danced over the snow.

*

The trail led across deserted streets and down silent alleys. The snow was falling faster now, and they had to shine the torch very low to the ground to pick up the rapidly filling footprints.

Eventually, Bright called a halt. 'It's no good,' he panted, 'we can't follow the tracks in this. That thing is too fast for us, and ...'

Off to their left they heard a sudden bellow of fright.

'Git outta here, ya pesky varmint – oh, ya wanna play hardball, huh?'

There was a sudden outburst of enraged squeaking.

John and Bright stared at each other and spoke simultaneously.

'Dodgy Dave!'

Dave's yard looked as if a whirlwind had been through it. Dave himself was sitting on the step in front of his office with his eyes and his mouth wide open. He was holding his stomach and making strange moaning noises. He turned an unfocused stare on to Bright. 'There was a b'ar.'

John looked puzzled. 'A bar?'

Bright clicked his tongue. 'He means a bear.' He turned to Dave. 'What happened?'

'I heard somethin' in my ration store, so I went to shoo it off, and it turned on me – biggest darn b'ar I ever saw. I was going to go and get my gun ...'

'You were going to shoot it?' cried Bright, horrified.

'Not with bullets – I got me one of those guns that fires anaesthetic darts, like they use to catch wild critturs.'

Bright breathed a sigh of relief. 'So where is my – I mean, where is this creature now?'

Dave shook his head. 'Search me. I never got to the gun. Darn crittur turned on me.'

Bright glared at him. 'You let it escape!'

Dave's jaw dropped. 'Let it escape?! That ol' boy head-butted me right in the guts! It would've torn me limb from limb if I hadn't kicked it on the snoot.'

Bright shook his head. 'You shouldn't have done that. You'll have made it angry.'

Dave snorted. 'It wasn't exactly friendly to start with.' He turned to John, his eyes narrowing. 'It didn't look like no b'ar I ever seen before. You guys know something about this thing?'

Bright nodded glumly. 'We'll have to find it before it kills somebody.'

'It wouldn't do that, would it?' John's voice was shocked. 'I mean, hamsters don't eat meat, do they? They eat nuts, and seeds, and … and …' John tailed off in the face of his ignorance about a hamster's diet.

'True.' Bright's voice was sombre. 'Hamsters are herbivores. But this isn't exactly a hamster any more, is it? It's got quite a lot of rat in it, and rats will eat anything. Besides, who knows what a hamster will eat if it's grown to hundreds of times its proper size and maddened with hunger?'

John stared at him. 'What are we going to do?'

'Stop it,' said Bright grimly, 'before it eats someone it shouldn't.'

CHAPTER EIGHT

The Hamster That Ate Birmingham

'*That was our Track from Way Back, "Jingle Bell Rock",
very seasonal for the time of year – now it's coming up
to nine thirty and time for the local news from Debbie.*'

After a night in which neither had slept much,
Bright and John were sitting in Bright's kitchen.
They were drinking hot chocolate and listening to
local radio which was now blasting out an urgent-
sounding jingle:

'*Wonderful Wham FM – News …*'

As the music faded, the announcer's voice came
in. '*Here is the Wham FM news at nine thirty, with me,
Debbie Williams. Listeners are ringing the Wham FM
newsdesk with reports of a strange creature on the*

loose in the Wham FM area. Local farmer Roy Boulton has a weird story. He says that overnight, a grain storage silo on his farm has been half emptied by a mysterious animal ...'

The announcer's breathless voice was replaced by the deeper tones of Farmer Boulton. 'I 'eard summat clatterin' round the feed bins, and there were this dirty great face come out at me, all eyes and whiskers. That must've been three metres tall, 'orrible it was, knocked me down flat an' scarpered off into the woods ...'

The announcer took up the story again. 'The police say they are keeping an open mind about the creature ...'

Bright switched the radio off and turned a haggard face to John. 'At least hamsters are nocturnal, so it's only been out in the night. I suppose that's why not many people have seen it yet.'

'That's all very well, but it's obviously still growing,' said John. 'How big is it going to get?'

Bright shrugged. 'I haven't a clue.'

'If it keeps getting bigger and bigger, it will start powering through buildings like a bulldozer.' John's imagination was going critical. 'It could destroy whole cities! You could go down in history as the person who created the Hamster That Ate Birmingham.'

'Calm down!' Bright's expression was pained. 'It can't possibly grow that big. Its skeleton wouldn't support it. Its body would collapse. I'm surprised it hasn't happened already.'

'Well, that's a relief. If its body collapses, all we'll have to worry about is a few tons of decomposing hamster! Where do you suppose it is now?'

'It's probably curled up asleep somewhere. It won't go out much in the daytime.' Bright looked out of the window. The snow had fallen all night. Now it was easing off, but the sky was still leaden with the promise of further falls.

John sat hunched at the table, the picture of misery. If only he hadn't found Frankenstein's notebook. If only he hadn't opened the box at Dodgy Dave's. He'd thought at the time about the evils that Pandora had let into the world by opening her box, but Pandora had nothing on him. There was a crazed giant hamster on the loose, and it was all his fault. Well, it was all Bright's fault, but it was all John's fault that it was all Bright's fault.

He sighed. 'I suppose we'd better go out and find it, if we can.' He reached for his scarf. 'The question is, if we do find it – what do we do then?'

Bright shook his head miserably. 'No idea.'

John and Bright spent the morning cycling around the town, scanning any open space that seemed big enough to hide the hamster. They'd poked around the old railway sidings and the disused shoe factory until they were chased off by irate security guards.

They called in for lunch at a fish and chip shop where a radio was squawking away in the corner. They listened to it as they queued.

'It's twelve thirty-five on wonderful Wham FM, and I'm joined now by Professor George Currell of the University of Middle England, and Nick Smelley ...'

'That's Smedleigh, Bob.'

'Sorry, Nick Smedleigh of the Institute for Paranormal Studies. Nick – is this strange creature just a figment of people's imaginations?'

'Well, Bob, it's been seen by a number of highly credible witnesses. Of course, the men of science will always close their minds to anything they don't understand ...'

'Thank you, Nick, and now if I can turn to George ...'

'Well, first let me say that the "Insititute for Paranormal Studies" is a pretty fancy name for a bunch of crackpots with zero scientific background who hold their meetings in Mr Smedleigh's spare bedroom ...'

'That's just the sort of blinkered pig-ignorance I'd expect from the scientific establishment ...'

'Well, sorry to stop you there, this argument clearly isn't over yet, but we're out of time, so here's another great song to put you in the mood for Christmas — "I Saw Mummy Kissing Santa Claus" ...'

Bright had reached the head of the queue.

'What'll it be, love?'

'Small portion of chips and a hamster please.'

'What?'

'Sorry, I meant small portion of chips and a haddock.'

After more hours of fruitless searching, John eyed the stark white landscape in despair. 'This is hopeless!'

He and Bright had spent the afternoon riding about the country lanes. They'd bumped over frozen tracks to check out the local woods. They'd poked around in barns. They were tired and cold and it was getting dark.

Bright nodded in agreement. 'We're getting nowhere. Let's go home.'

On their way, they passed a tractor and trailer that had run off the road into a ditch, spilling its load of turnips. A police car stood beside it with its blue lights flashing.

'So let's get this straight,' a policeman was saying to a shaken farmworker. 'You were on your way back to the farm when you heard a munching noise, you turned round and you saw an extremely large mouse eating your turnips.'

'No. It was a hamster,' said the farmworker.

'A hamster,' repeated the policeman.

The man nodded. 'That's right.'

'Just blow hard into this tube, would you, sir?'

John opened his mouth to say something. Bright elbowed him in the ribs. 'Don't even try to explain,' he hissed.

'But it might be somewhere near by!'

Bright shook his head. 'It'll be miles away by now. Anyway, it can see in the dark – we can't.'

John nodded glumly and pushed off. His bike, and Bright's, slithered on the icy road surface.

Hidden deep in a thicket, Mister Nibbles watched them go. There was something familiar about the two-legged creature with spiky fur. Mister Nibbles had a dim idea that Spiky-fur hadn't treated him kindly. His black eyes glittered dangerously.

It was fully dark by the time they arrived back at Bright's house. John filled the kettle while Bright switched the radio on.

'That was Nat King Cole and "The Little Boy That Santa Claus Forgot". More seasonal good cheer later, but right now it's over to Wham FM's Traffic Update with Mike November.'

'Well, there have been a lot of minor bumps in these difficult driving conditions, but the police say that the gritters have been out and all major routes are open. We've just had a call from a Wham FM listener – Don

from Diddington says he's just seen a giant hamster rush straight across a main road and squash two vans flat, leaving their drivers badly shaken. What d'you think of that, Terry?'

'Well, Mike, there's something I'd like to say to Don from Diddington – pull over, mate, you're in no condition to drive ...!'

Bright switched the radio off again.

John stared at him. 'Did they say it squashed two vans flat?'

'Hmmm.'

'It must be huge!' John wrung his hands. 'We can't tackle a thing that size.'

'No, we can't,' said Bright. 'But I know a man who can.'

'No way!'

'Look, Dave, it's perfectly simple. We go back to where we know the hamster's been seen, we track it down and you shoot it with that anaesthetic dart gun of yours. Then we can wrap it up in one of your camouflage nets.'

'Sounds a great plan except for one tiny flaw. Guess what that is.'

Bright gave Dodgy Dave a hard stare. 'You told

me you fought in Vietnam with the US Marines.'

'I also told you I fought at the Alamo. Sue me.'

'You owe me a favour.'

Dave was unmoved. 'No, I don't.'

'Well, do this and I'll owe you a favour.'

'En–oh spells no!'

'Please, Dave,' begged John, 'you've got to help us.'

'Ain't no *got to* about it,' grumbled Dave. 'You boys got yourselves into this mess, you get yourselves out of it.'

Bright's face took on a cunning expression. 'Oh dear. Then I suppose Mister Nibbles will go berserk and cause untold damage, and the police and the army will be called in and they'll find out that I got most of the equipment for my experiments from your yard.'

A look of panic began to dawn on Dave's face. 'Now, just a cotton-pickin' minute …'

'And then they'll come poking around and find all sorts of brand-new top-secret rocket guidance systems and things that shouldn't be here.'

Dave's shoulders slumped in defeat. 'OK, OK – I'll do it! You boys get the net, and I'll get the dart gun. We're goin' hamster huntin'.'

Dave's jeep screeched to a halt in the country lane. The tractor and trailer had been pulled out of the ditch, and towed away, but the gap in the hedge showed where they had been.

Bright shone his torch into the ditch. 'He's been back here,' he said.

John looked down. 'How can you tell?'

'The tractor that crashed here was towing a load of turnips, right?' John nodded. 'Well, where are they?'

John looked around. No turnips. 'Maybe the people from the farm loaded them back on the trailer.'

'Possibly,' said Bright, 'but that doesn't explain

why there's a hamster pellet over there the size of a Volkswagen.' He shone his torch on to the gently steaming dropping.

Bright was exaggerating – the dropping wasn't really much bigger than a kid's pedal car, but it was still pretty impressive for a hamster. Dave joined them and whistled. 'This baby must be one big enchilada.'

Bright shone his torch away from the site of the hamster's turnip-eating orgy. A clear trail led away across the frozen fields.

Without another word, they set off to follow it; Bright with his torch, Dave with the stun gun, and John with the net, and deep misgivings.

Before long, they came to a wooded hillside. In front of them, a track led through a gap in the hills. The track had been closed by a steel gate, but this now lay broken and twisted to one side.

'I know where we are,' John hissed. 'That track leads to Mousehole Quarry.'

Bright gave a mirthless grin. 'Very appropriate.'

The hamster's pawprints led straight up the track, disappearing through a gap in the trees into the heart of the hill.

'OK.' Dave became very businesslike. 'We'll enter that there de-file in skirmishing order. Vernie, you take point.' He turned to John. 'You take flank. Circle round to the south and create a diversion.'

'I have an even more brilliant military strategy for degrading the enemy's offensive capability.' Bright paused impressively. 'We all sneak up on it, you shoot it, we net it.'

'Nice plan.'

'Come on.'

In the summer, the quarry was a favourite, but forbidden, playground for the local kids. The reason it was forbidden was that part of the workings were flooded, forming a pool of unknown depth, glassy-surfaced and deadly. Now the pool was covered by a thick coating of ice and snow, so it was impossible to spot if you didn't know it was there.

Tonight, the quarry lay quiet and empty in the silver-blue light of the moon. Dave crept forward. Behind him tiptoed Bright and John, net at the ready. They gazed over the unbroken snow.

'Gee, nobody home, what a shame.' Dave shrugged. 'C'mon, let's go.'

There was a rustle from their right. Dave turned slowly. John and Bright dropped the net from nerveless fingers. They watched spellbound as a pile of brushwood against the quarry face heaved. A twitching nose poked out. A pair of midnight-black eyes peered menacingly across at them.

'Jee-hoshaphat!' Dave's teeth started clicking like castanets.

John said, in a voice that seemed to belong to someone else, 'It's grown a bit since last night.'

SQUEAK!

Mister Nibbles thrust aside the remainder of his bedding (mostly young fir trees) and reared up on his hind legs. His misshapen body with its patchwork coat loomed higher and higher until it blotted out the stars.

'Well, if that ain't a sight to make a man mess his pants,' breathed Dave.

The hamster stood well over ten metres tall.

'Stun it!' hissed Bright.

Dave looked down at the gun in his hands. 'With this? You couldn't stun it with a bazooka!'

Perhaps Mister Nibbles recognized his creator, and was overcome with a lust for revenge. Perhaps he just didn't take kindly to being woken up. With an ear-splitting squeak of fury, the hamster charged.

It was over in a moment. Dave dropped his rifle and turned to run. A cuff from one huge paw sent him flying; he bounced off a tree and lay stunned on the ground.

Bright stood transfixed with horror as Mister Nibbles scooped him up between his forepaws. The hamster sat back on its haunches and held Bright up. It sniffed at him, making a noise like a thousand vacuum cleaners.

John stared in horrified fascination. Mister Nibbles was holding Bright just as if he was a

sunflower seed. And any second now, he would start nibbling at Bright, starting at his head. I always knew Bright was some kind of nut, John thought.

Bright had evidently had the same thought. 'Help meeee!' he screeched.

John leapt to Dave's gun, pointed it wildly towards the hamster, and pulled the trigger. There was a loud *pop*, and the gun jerked violently; John dropped it and wrung his fingers. The dart went nowhere near the hamster, but slammed into the rockface just below the rim of the quarry. Mister Nibbles gave a deafening squeak and dropped Bright, who rolled away shrieking. John gazed in open-mouthed horror as the enraged beast turned to face him and prepared to charge.

Maybe it was the impact of the dart. Maybe it was the hamster's roar of fury. Whatever the cause, at that moment, the snow piled up on the steep slope above the quarry began to move. The hamster gave a squeak of alarm and turned round just in time for the resulting avalanche to hit it smack in the face. With a thunderous roar, hundreds of tons of snow cascaded over Mister Nibbles, burying him completely.

The blast from the avalanche had knocked John to the ground. He picked himself up and stared for a moment, breathing deeply. Then he shook himself and went over to check his companions. Dave was staggering to his feet, bleeding from a cut on the temple. Bright was half-covered in powdered snow, and as pale as a ghost. He was clutching at his ankle.

'Sprained,' he hissed through gritted teeth.

Dave took a look and nodded. 'We'd better find you a medic, fella. I'll bring the jeep up.' He looked across the quarry to the huge mound of snow covering Mister Nibbles. 'Well, that was kind of improvised, but I guess you'd call it a result.' He limped off to fetch the jeep.

John dragged Bright's left arm across his shoulders and helped him to stand. Grimacing with pain, Bright hopped slowly towards the entrance to the quarry.

'Don't say it,' he muttered.

'Say what?'

'Don't say that none of this would have happened if I hadn't tried mucking about with the secret of life itself.'

'All right, I won't.'

'And you can stop thinking it, as well. Would it help if I said I was sorry?'

John shrugged.

'I'm sorry. There. Did that help?'

From behind them came a noise, something between a creak and a rumble. John spun round; Bright staggered, putting weight on his damaged ankle.

'Ow! What d'you think you're …?' Bright looked back the way they'd come. His jaw dropped. 'Oh no!'

The mound of snow covering Mister Nibbles had begun to move. A very large pink nose appeared and began sniffing. Whiskers sprang clear of the snow and began to twitch.

John turned his back on the dazed hamster and broke into a shambling run, half dragging Bright away from the quarry. 'Come on!'

Bright hopped madly to keep up. 'I'm – ow – coming – ow –'

Dave's jeep bounced into view along the track. John saw his expression change as his headlights picked up the hamster's struggles to free itself. He slewed the jeep round in a skid-turn and sat revving the engine.

'Get in here,' yelled Dave. 'Watcha waitin' for?'

With the last of his strength, John heaved Bright over the tailboard into the back of the jeep, and piled in after him, just as Mister Nibbles shrugged free of the snow.

The hamster's very, very big black eyes had a deadly gleam. Having cold, wet stuff thrown at it was the last straw! The hamster wasn't going to take all this lying down. No more Mister Nice Nibbles!

Dave slammed the jeep into gear. The wheels spun on the icy ground. John peered over the tailgate and gave a moan of terror as several tons of furry death charged. The earth shook.

Just as the jeep began to move, the hamster was upon them. Lying on his back, John looked up into two nostrils like tunnel mouths, front teeth like pickaxes, a tongue like a wobbly red mattress – and kicked out in panic, catching Mister Nibbles a hefty whack on the snout. The hamster blinked. Its squeak became a snarl.

With one paw it scooped John from the back of the jeep …

… and stuffed him into one enormous cheek pouch.

Bright tapped Dave on the shoulder. 'The hamster's eaten John …'

'Don't bother me with details,' yelled Dave. 'Duck!'

He dodged down behind the dashboard. The jeep shot under the trunk of a fallen tree, tearing its windscreen off in the process. Bright sat up just in time to see the hamster plough through the tree as if it wasn't there.

'He's right behind us! Go faster,' he croaked. 'We must go faster …'

The Christmas Fair in the Parish of Itsnotte had been a local attraction since 1493.

Among the revellers tonight were Ms Session and Mr Hardman. In spite of the temperature, the PE teacher was dressed in jeans and a cap-sleeved shirt. He was still limping from his self-defence session with Bright, but his face was glowing with good health and cheap aftershave.

Ms Session had managed to drag him away from the shooting gallery (and the coconut shy and the test-your-strength machine and the wrestling booth), and the evening seemed to be looking up.

'Ooh, look,' she said, pointing at a huge

glittering structure like a giant spider web. 'A Ferris wheel! I wouldn't mind a go on that, Rodney.'

Mr Hardman shuddered, but only said, 'Right you are, Viv.'

He felt in his pocket for money.

'What's it doing?'

A safe distance ahead of the hamster, Dave brought the jeep to a halt. Mister Nibbles seemed to have given up the pursuit and was standing in the middle of the road, his nose turned towards a glow in the sky. The sounds of thumping rock music and the cries of the showmen rose in the still night air.

Mister Nibbles blinked. He didn't like lights and loud noises, but his dim hamster brain recalled happy hours of exercise on a big, round thing in his cage, just like the one he could see down there.

It's possible that John, wriggling, drenched in hamster slobber and half suffocated inside Mister Nibbles' cheek pouch, would have been even more miserable if he'd known exactly what the hamster had in mind, but possibly not.

Bright and Dave watched in horror as the hamster padded away from the road, and towards the bright lights below.

Bright pointed dramatically. 'We've got to get John back.'

Dave nodded. 'Yup. We don't leave our people in there.'

'Follow that hamster!'

'Wheee! This is fun!' Ms Session clapped her hands and laughed as their car reached the top of the wheel and rocked as it started the descent.

Mr Hardman, who had a terrible fear of heights he would have died rather than admit to, gave a fixed grin and said, 'Yeah, right!'

Ms Session gave him a sideways glance. 'You're

not – scared, are you?'

'Me? Nah, whatever gave you that idea?' Mr Hardman gripped the safety bar tighter.

'Silly boy.' Ms Session reached across and stroked Mr Hardman's straining knuckles. 'You're safe with me.'

Mr Hardman turned to face her. 'Oh, Viv!'

'Oh, Rodney!'

'Oh, Viv!'

'Oh – hang on a minute.' Ms Session pulled away from her companion and said, 'Is it my imagination or is this wheel going faster?'

Mr Hardman looked around and felt his mouth go dry as the fairground flashed past. Also, there seemed to be a thundering noise every time the wheel swept close to the ground.

As the car started its next climb, a giant furry bottom flashed before their startled eyes. Ms Session gazed down as the car continued its rocket-like ascent.

'Don't look now,' she said tightly, 'but there's a ten-metre-long hamster using this ride as an exercise wheel.'

Everyone on the Ferris wheel started to scream. Mr Hardman screamed the loudest of the lot.

Horn blasting and engine roaring, Dave's jeep bucketed through the fairground, scattering the crowd. It juddered to a halt in front of the Ferris wheel. Dave piled out.

The man who ran the ride was tearing his hair out. 'Somebody stop it!' he yelled. 'It's not designed to go this fast – the bearings are running red hot! The whole thing'll collapse in a minute!'

By now, Dave's body was awash with adrenalin. With a whoop, he fished around in the back of the jeep and hauled out a plastic bucket full of yellow sticks. 'Yeeeehhhhaaaaa! Let's see how that ol' boy likes these apples!'

From the back of the jeep, Bright stared at him in apprehension. 'What have you got there?

Dave grinned like a maniac. 'Distress flares.' He selected a stick and held it in both hands, pointed at the hamster. 'Stay back, amigo.'

Bright hauled himself into a sitting position. 'Don't do that!' he squeaked. 'You'll make it …'

Dave shot the flare, which exploded above the hamster's head. It gave a blood-curdling squeak of rage and fright.

'… angry.'

Mister Nibbles stopped running and reared up. The Ferris wheel shuddered to a sudden stop, sending the cars tumbling in stomach-churning somersaults.

The smoke from the flare was clearly irritating the hamster. It pawed frantically at its nose and took several deep breaths.

A – A – AACHOOO – EEK!

A small, moist figure shot out of the hamster's mouth.

Ms Session flung her arms around Mr Hardman as their car wobbled to a halt.

'Oh, Rodney, are you all right?'

Mr Hardman's face was a peculiar shade of green, but he did his best to stick his chest out. 'Oh, yes, course, Viv. Don't worry, you're safe with me.'

'Oh, Rodney.'

'Oh, Viv …'

'Oh, Rodney …'

'Ohhhh helllllpppppppp …!'

The car rocked as someone damp and sticky landed in their laps.

'Oh, sorry,' said John.

Onlookers screamed and ran as the hamster tumbled out of the wheel and blundered into an overhead cable dotted with coloured lamps. There was an almighty shower of sparks, a loud pop and all the lights in the fairground went out.

It was several minutes before the fairground staff were able to restore power. During that time, John managed to extricate himself from the Ferris wheel and rejoin Bright and Dave.

The lights flickered on, revealing a damaged but hamsterless fairground. Mister Nibbles had completely disappeared.

CHAPTER TEN

Goodbye, Mister-Nibbles?

Mousehole Quarry was quiet. Flurries of snow split the night air. The armoured car came to a rest. Dave switched off the engine.

The hamster hunters looked out into the darkness.

Dave's voice broke the silence. *"Twas the night before Christmas and all through the house, Not a creature was stirring, not even a mouse ...* or a giant homicidal hamster ...'

'Oh, very droll,' said Bright.

'Just tryin' to lighten the mood, homeboy ...'

Bright, John and Dave had rushed back to the yard

121

from the fair. Dave had strapped Bright's leg up with unexpected competence. Now Bright was hopping around quite freely, using a ski-pole to help him balance. He was still demanding that Mister Nibbles should be captured alive, but gave the impression that he was ready to consider other options.

Dave, on the other hand, had decided that it was time to 'bring out the big guns'. He'd cleared junk away from around his armoured car. Then he'd packed the cramped interior with an arsenal of weapons. There were a variety of bazookas, anti-tank missiles and strange-looking tubes that John had only ever seen in sci-fi films. Just to show he really meant business, he'd also taken off his jacket and ripped a strip of cloth from his singlet, which he tied round his forehead. John hadn't been impressed.

'Who does he think he is? Rambo?'

'More like Dumbo,' muttered Bright.

At last, Dave had climbed into the car, snapped on a pair of goggles and gripped the gear stick. 'Ready to rumble? Wagons roll!'

With lights blazing, the armoured car had sped off into the night …

Nothing moved in the quarry. No sound broke the stillness.

'Do you think it's in there?' whispered John.

Bright nodded. 'Trust me.'

Dave sighed. 'You just had to go and say that, didn't you?' He took a thermos flask from under his seat and poured out a mug of strong black coffee.

'OK, here's the plan,' he drawled, putting the mug down beside the gear lever. 'I stay here and set up the welcoming party. You go in there and drive the critter out. Then, kapow!'

He broke off as, from out of the darkness, came a muffled *boom*.

John's teeth started to chatter. 'Did anyone hear that?'

Another *boom*.

Dave was staring at his coffee mug.

Another *boom*.

A ripple spread across the black surface of the liquid.

Boom.

Ripple.

Boom.

Ripple.

Dave cleared his throat. 'I think we got company.'

Hardly daring to breathe, John helped the limping Bright out of the armoured vehicle. Dave flicked on the vehicle's searchlight. It shone into the dark sky, barely making an impression on the cloud-covered night. John looked around nervously.

Bright hopped over to John, nudged him and pointed. To their left, small fir trees lay strewn along the ground like giant toothpicks. Their branches had been stripped clean off. Taking his weight on the ski-pole, Bright bent down and examined the trunks. Giant toothmarks were clearly visible.

'He's in there,' whispered Bright.

A flap on the armoured car creaked open and a pair of anxious eyes peered out. 'Be alert and watch for incoming hamsters,' hissed Dave helpfully.

At that moment there was a break in the clouds and moonlight came pouring down.

SQUUEAAKKKKK!!!!!!!!

John, Bright and Dave screamed in unison as the

hamster leapt out from the quarry. The moon outlined a nightmarish vision. Giant paws raised and teeth bared, the hamster lurched forward and charged straight for the armoured car.

'Take cover!' yelled Bright.

He and John dived to the ground as a paw crashed into the side of the armoured car, flipping it upside down.

'Dave,' yelled John, 'get out of there!'

CRACK!

The car split open like a walnut. The hamster

raised itself up and gave another bloodcurdling squeak.

Dave crawled out of the shattered heap of metal a split second before another titanic blow flattened the car completely. Squeaking with triumph, the hamster jumped up and down on the wreckage while Dave broke the world record for the twenty-metre-crawl.

'Holeee-heck!' he moaned. 'Ma pride and joy! The only thing it's good for now is maple syrup. It's been pancaked.'

'What are we going to do?' wailed John as the hamster turned and sniffed the air.

'Retreat!' screamed Dave as he began slipping and sliding away from danger.

John tried to follow, but tripped over one of the discarded tree trunks. The hamster staggered towards him. John was rooted to the spot. He was going to be squashed flat and there was nothing he could do about it. Dealing with an attack by a hamster the size of a house had not been a topic featured in Mr Hardman's self-defence classes.

Mr Hardman! Self defence! A light suddenly shone through the darkness of John's despair. What had Bright used to throw the PE teacher across the gym? 'Akido!' he screamed at Bright. 'Use your Akido on it!'

Bright stared at him. 'What?'

'You said you could turn an opponent's strength against him. You said "the bigger they are, the harder they fall!"'

'That thing is ten metres tall!' yelled Bright. 'There are limits!'

The light in John's mind blew a fuse. Despair flooded back as warm hamster slobber fell on his head for the second time that night. This is it, John thought.

'Hey! Fuzzface!'

A ski-pole bounced off the hamster's back. It turned away from John. Bright stood before it, waving a broken tree branch.

'Come on, Mister Nibbles! You may be a monstrous, demonic, nightmare creature from the darkest pit of hell, but you don't scare me!' Bright threw the branch. The hamster swatted it away.

'I knew you when you were just a small ball of fur!'

The hamster roared. Several small trees fell over.

'Come and get me then,' demanded Bright as he limped away from the enraged hamster.

John scrambled to his feet and watched in horror as Mister Nibbles stomped after Bright.

Bright broke into a limping trot. The hamster followed suit. The moon lit up the two figures as they surged through the quarry workings. John raced after them, but not too quickly. He didn't really want to catch them up.

The chase led towards the frozen quarry pool. Beneath the snow, ice glinted in the moonlight. Bright reached the edge of the pool and turned to face his pursuer.

'Follow the leader!' he cried and stepped out on to the frozen surface of the water.

The hamster followed.

John slithered to an icy halt at the pool's edge. 'No!' he yelled. 'It's too dangerous!'

His warning went unheeded. John stood looking on helplessly as 'creator' and 'created' slithered and slipped across the white surface, further and further away from the safety of solid ground, towards the middle of the pool.

Bright stopped and turned to face the hamster.

It roared, sending snow swirling around in a white maelstrom as it moved in for the kill …

At that moment, Bright heard a small, splitting

sound coming from beneath the hamster's feet. He smiled. 'The game is over, Mister Nibbles,' he whispered.

Ice groaned under the weight of the hamster. Jagged fissures appeared, followed in quick succession by a series of ear-splitting cracks. Sheets of ice splintered into a thousand shards and water began to shoot upwards through the broken surface. Bright was hurled from his feet.

The hamster twisted and turned in fear and confusion as it crashed downwards through the ice.

SQUEEAAAAAAAAAAK!

The hamster was sucked into the cold waters of the quarry. Its giant paws scrabbled uselessly at the ice; cold water clung to its fur, froze immediately, and dragged it down. Even the creature's immense strength was no help in fighting the added weight of the clinging ice. Slowly and surely, the hamster sank into the black icy depths.

After the explosion of noise, all that could be heard was the gurgling of bubbles as they rose to the surface. After that there was silence.

John felt an intoxicating cocktail of emotions: waves of fear, horror, relief and worry surged through him.

He suddenly realized that he couldn't see Bright. Had he been sucked down into the pool as well? Tears began to pour down his cheeks. The freezing night air turned them into little pearls of ice.

'Bright!' he called out. 'Where are you!'

'I'm here!'

John's heart leapt as he heard the faint but familiar voice. He peered into the darkness and was just able to make out the figure of Bright clinging on to a sheet of ice.

'Hang on, Bright. I'll get you out!' he yelled. 'But how?' he moaned to himself.

'We could use this here lasso.'

John turned. Dodgy Dave stood behind him, holding a length of rope.

'I thought you'd run away,' exclaimed John.

'No way, José!' replied Dave. 'That was tactics. I was goin' for help. I'd have been back with the cavalry in no time at all. I did somethin' similar for General Custer at the Battle of Little Bighorn.'

John looked puzzled. 'Weren't Custer and all his men killed?'

'I got back late …'

'HELP!'

'This is no time to start relivin' past times! Let's get the critter out!'

Within minutes, Bright sat on the pool's edge, teeth chattering, wrapped in a blanket that Dave had managed to salvage from the wrecked armoured car. Ice covered his hair, making it look like upside-down icicles. A frosty sheen covered his face.

'Heck,' drawled Dave, 'I know you should put ice on a sprained ankle, dude, but that is taking it to the extreme.'

'H–h–h–has it gone?' chattered Bright.

'Yes,' replied John. 'It's gone ...'

It was late afternoon on Christmas Eve before John was able to visit Bright to check up on his health. He found him in his lab, with his ankle strapped up, listening to the radio.

'Hello, Bright!' he called. 'Have you heard ...?'

'Sssh!' Bright gave him an impatient wave and turned the volume up.

'This is WHAM FM wishing you an aitch–ai–pee–pee–why Christmas with snowballs on. Back with me in the studio are Professor George Currell and Nick Smedleigh. George, Nick, are yesterday's sightings

131

further evidence of the existence of giant hamsters?'

'Absolutely, Bob, as you say, further evidence ...'

'Just a minute, Mr Smedleigh, there is no PROPER evidence; no pictures, no video footage ...'

'We have the word of many people, including some local teachers ...'

'As I said, no PROPER evidence ... Bob, this is just a simple case of panic-induced hallucination. One person thinks they've seen a giant hamster and the next thing you know, everyone wants to have seen one! It's mass hysteria brought on by people indulging in a little too much Christmas spirit!'

'With due respect, surely the simple explanation is

that if people say they saw a ten-metre-tall hamster,
then they did see a ten-metre-tall hamster?'

'With absolutely no respect, science doesn't
recognize ten-metre-tall hamsters ...'

'You'd recognize one if it sat on you ...'

'Wouldn't.'

'Would.'

'Wouldn't.'

John smiled as the 'scientific debate' continued.
Thank goodness for science! Soon Mister Nibbles
would be just a memory; an urban myth, a story
told that no one would ever believe ...

'Thanks for that high-level debate, gents. This is
WHAM FM and here's a goodie to put in your Christmas
stocking: the brand-new rave techno version of that old
classic carol, "Good King Wenceslas" ...'

'Good King Wenceslas
Looked out, out, out, out, out, out, out ... ...'

Bright grunted in disgust and turned the radio
off.

'I'm glad you're OK,' said John. 'Which is more
than I'll be when I have to tell Ms Session ...'

Bright smirked. 'Don't worry. You'll be able to
blackmail her – just mention the fact that you saw

her and Mr Hardman together on the Ferris wheel. That should do it. You know how teachers are about their private lives.'

'Good idea.'

'I'm full of them,' replied Bright.

'How's the ankle?'

'I've been ordered to take it easy for a few days. The doctor says I've just got a minor sprain. Though what that doctor knows is nothing. I've torn my medial deltoid ligament ...'

John nodded. Bright, as usual, knew best.

'One thing I've been meaning to ask you,' said John. 'What gave you the idea to lure Mister Nibbles into the middle of the pool?'

'It was you! Use Akido, you said. So I did.'

John looked puzzled.

'Remember the philosophy? Make the opponent's strength its weakness. The hamster's size and weight were its strength. The ice made those strengths into weaknesses. Simple really.'

John looked on in admiration. 'You knew the ice would break! Did you work it out scientifically, you know, estimating Mister Nibbles' weight and the thickness of the ice and all that clever sort of stuff you do?'

Bright gave a cough. 'Well, I could have. Actually, I wasn't at all sure it would work. I didn't have any figures for the forces involved. How could I?'

John's jaw dropped. 'But what if it hadn't worked? What if …?' His question was left hanging in the air.

'Anyway, no harm done!'

'No harm done?' exploded John. 'No harm done?' He then proceeded to tell Bright what harm *had* been done.

It took him some time.

Eventually, he dropped the final bombshell. 'Where is Frankenstein's notebook?' he demanded.

Bright pointed to the side. John hurried over and picked it up.

'It has to be destroyed.'

'What!'

'You heard me. I found it. Dave gave it to me. It's caused too many problems. I want it destroyed.'

Bright was horrified. 'But it's the most important scientific document in the history of the world! It can't be destroyed. I don't have any serum left!'

'Good!'

'But what about mankind? They need this!'

'They don't need ten-metre-tall hamsters. Nature shouldn't be messed with.' John was not going to be persuaded otherwise. 'Where are the matches …?'

John pulled over a metal wastepaper bin. He held the pages above it and set fire to them, one by one. Throughout the operation, Bright sat groaning and moaning as he grieved for his loss.

Soon all that was left of Victor Frankenstein's notebook was a pile of charred ashes.

Pandora's box is finally closed, thought John. He turned to Bright. 'Right, got to go. Don't bother getting up, I'll see myself out. Merry Christmas!' He waved a cheery goodbye and left.

Bright waited until he heard the front door slam shut, then he hopped over to his desk. He opened a drawer and took out a sheaf of paper. Bright flicked through the first couple of sheets. They were full of familiar-looking writing and diagrams. A wolf-like grin appeared across Bright's face.

Hadn't John ever heard of photocopying? …

Back home, John slumped on the sofa and reached for the TV remote. He flicked through the channels. Soap ... soap ... soap ... soap ...

On one of the satellite channels, he found a wildlife documentary. He checked the TV guide. Here it was, *Life in Santa's Garden* – 'a seasonal look at creatures of the Arctic'. John sighed, Well, at least it wasn't a soap.

The screen showed a snowy wilderness. A breathless American voice intoned, *'Winter in the Arctic: a time for all of nature to slow down. While Santa and his little helpers'* (John yawned) *'are busy making presents for all good little boys and girls, several of the creatures in Santa's garden are curling up for a six-month snooze.'*

I could do with a six-month snooze, thought John sleepily.

'As temperatures fall, their body clocks slow down until they are almost frozen in time.'

Frozen in time, breathed John dreamily.

'Some creatures are even able to survive for many years, in suspended animation, locked in the ice.'

Locked in the ice. The words ran through John's mind. How strange it must be, to lie suspended between life and death. Calm. Peaceful. *Waiting* ...

'... until the spring thaw, when they suddenly come back to life.'

John sat bolt upright. The pond in the quarry wouldn't be frozen for ever. What if …?

The picture of a thawing pool rose in his mind – the waters warming, bubbles floating to the surface, a huge shape rising from the depths …

He gripped the sofa cushion. A cold sweat flooded his brow. He gasped for breath.

A strange cry echoed across the snow-muffled roofs of the town …